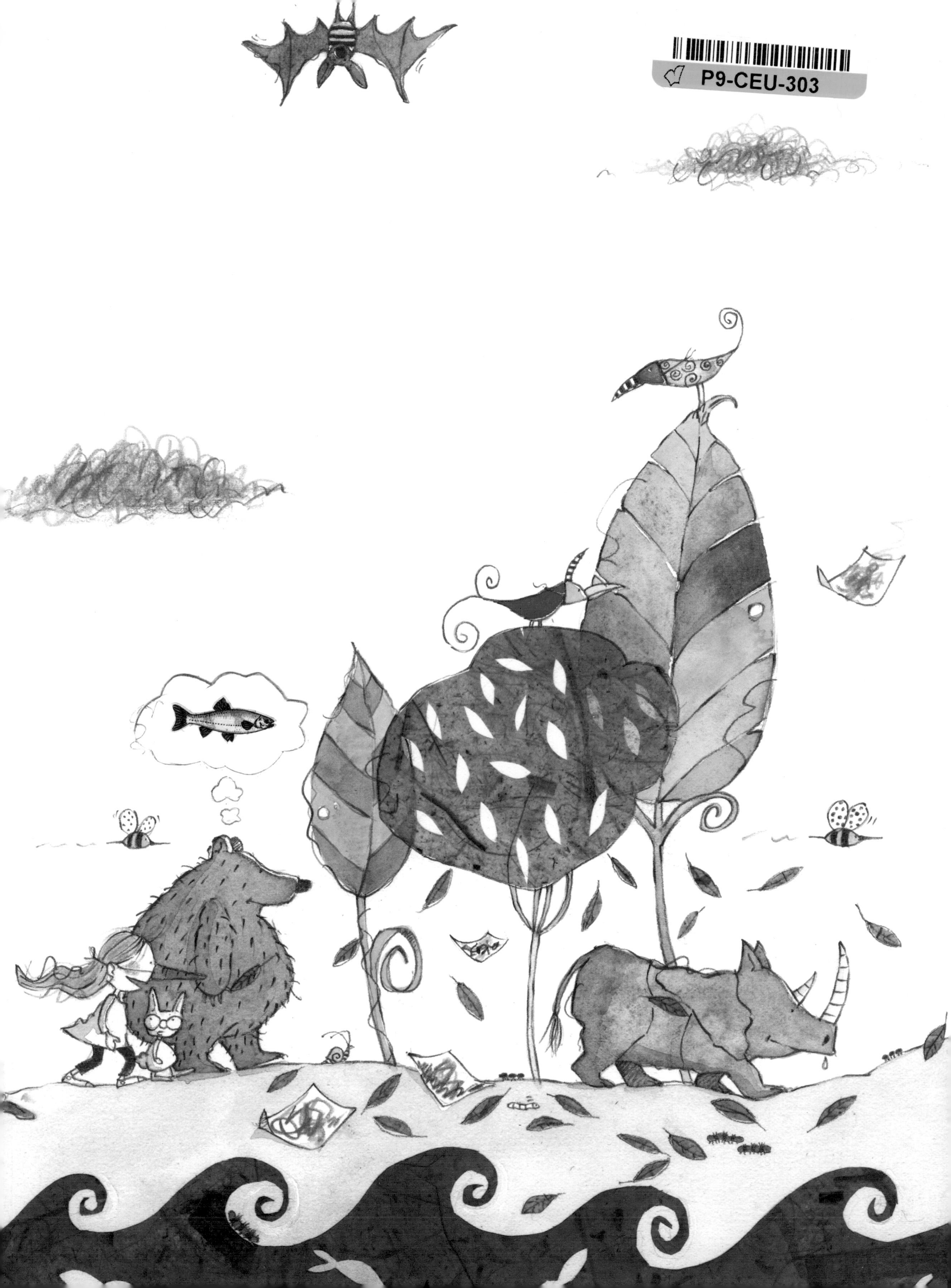

Published in Canada and the USA in 2017 by Groundwood Books

Groundwood Books / House of Anansi Press
groundwoodbooks.com

We acknowledge for their financial support of our publishing program the Canada Council for the Arts, the Ontario Arts Council and the Government of Canada.

Canada Council for the Arts | Conseil des Arts du Canada

ONTARIO ARTS COUNCIL
CONSEIL DES ARTS DE L'ONTARIO
an Ontario government agency
un organisme du gouvernement de l'Ontario

With the participation of the Government of Canada
Avec la participation du gouvernement du Canada | Canada

Library and Archives Canada Cataloguing in Publication
Gay, Marie-Louise, author, illustrator
Short stories for little monsters / Marie-Louise Gay.
Short stories.
ISBN 978-1-55498-896-9 (hardback)
I. Title.
PS8563.A868S56 2017 jC813'.54 C2016-904227-8

The illustrations were done in watercolor, ink, colored pencil, 6B pencil and collage, using Japanese and Italian paper.
Design by Michael Solomon
Printed and bound in Malaysia

FSC www.fsc.org
MIX
Paper from responsible sources
FSC® C012700

SHORT STORIES FOR LiTTLE MONSTERS

MARIE-LouiSE GAY

GROUNDWOOD BOOKS   HOUSE OF ANANSI PRESS   TORONTO   BERKELEY

For Lucie P.

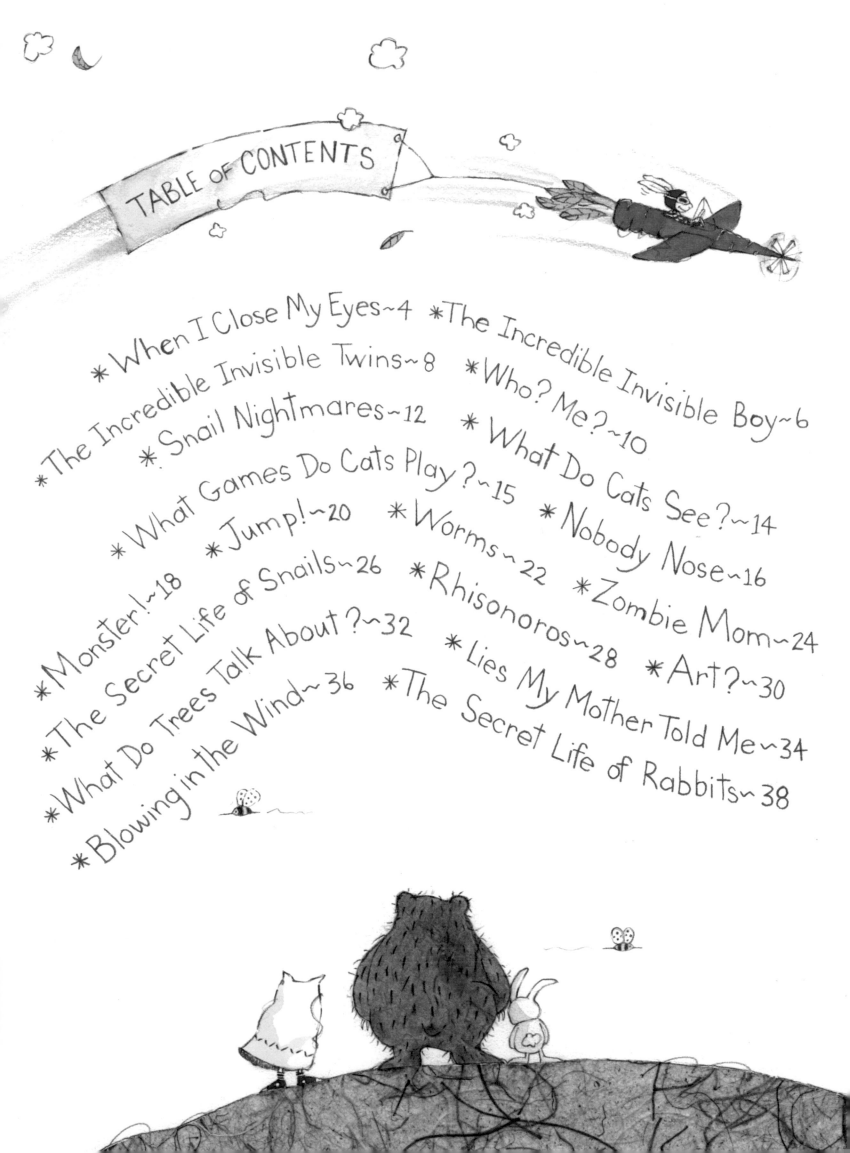

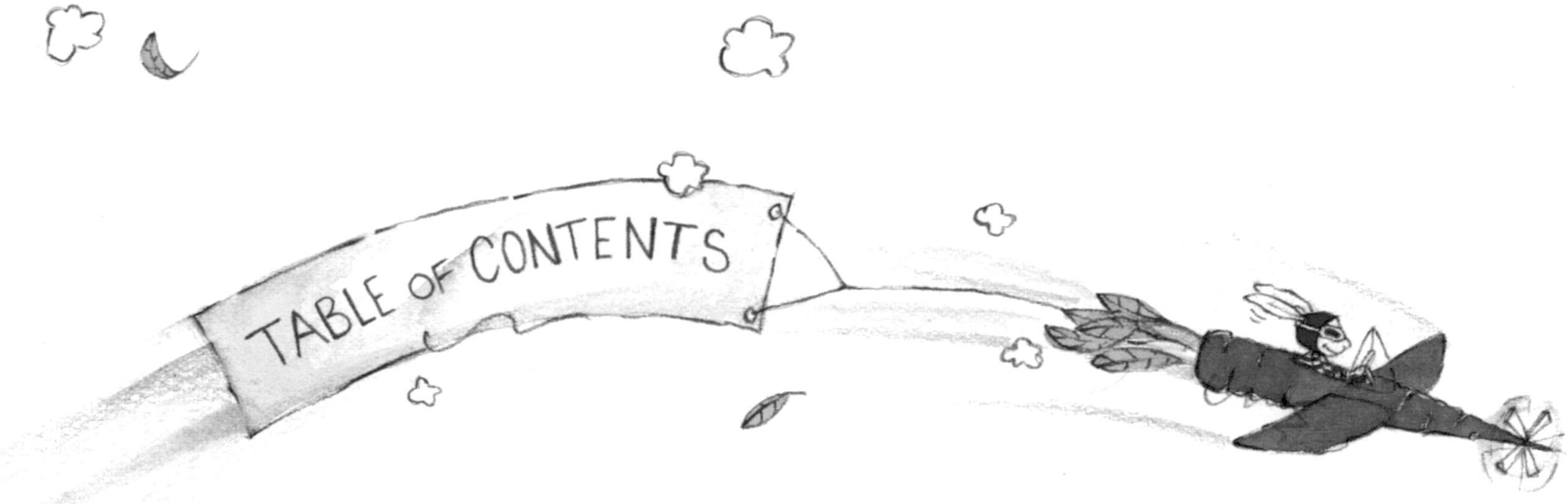
TABLE OF CONTENTS

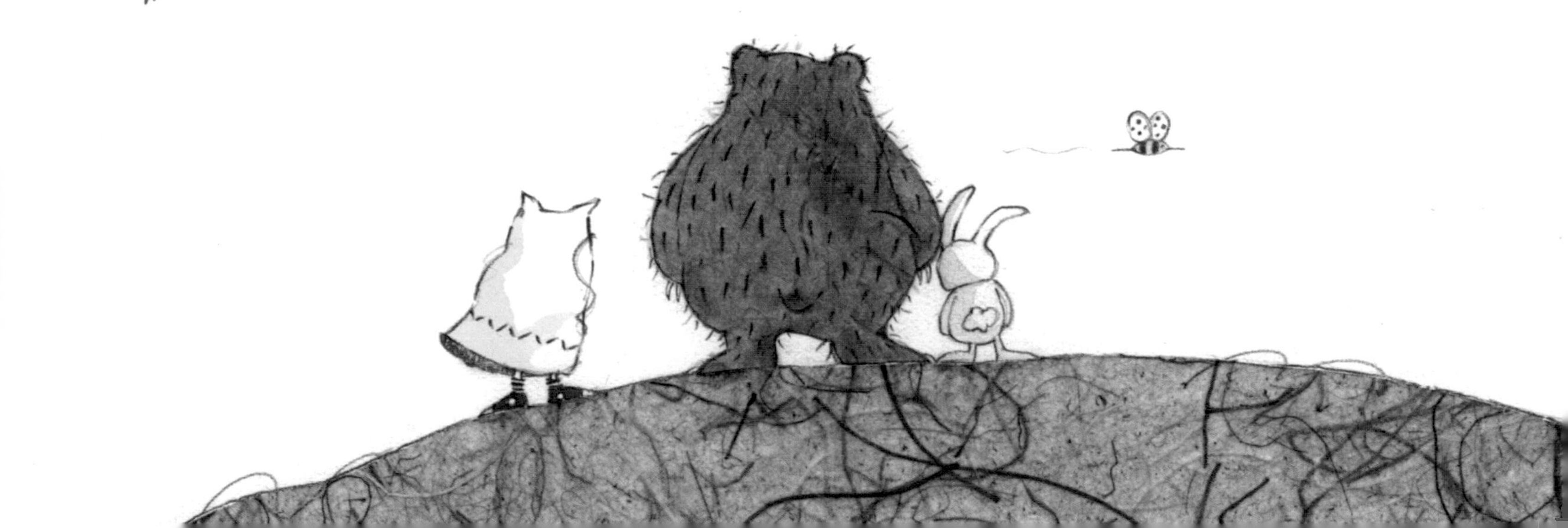

WHEN I CLOSE MY EYES

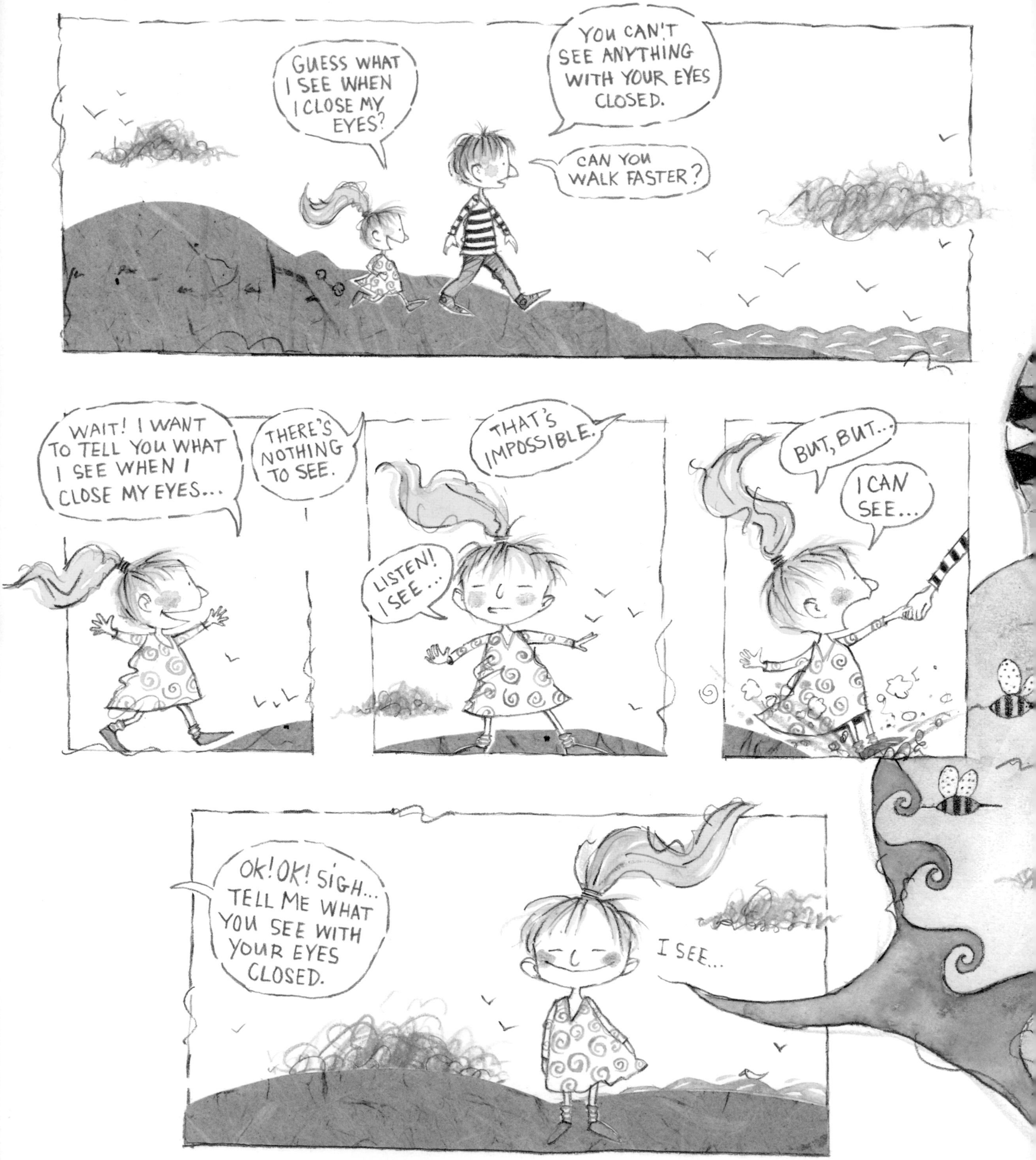
GUESS WHAT I SEE WHEN I CLOSE MY EYES?
YOU CAN'T SEE ANYTHING WITH YOUR EYES CLOSED.
CAN YOU WALK FASTER?
WAIT! I WANT TO TELL YOU WHAT I SEE WHEN I CLOSE MY EYES...
THERE'S NOTHING TO SEE.
THAT'S IMPOSSIBLE.
LISTEN! I SEE...
BUT, BUT...
I CAN SEE...
OK! OK! SIGH... TELL ME WHAT YOU SEE WITH YOUR EYES CLOSED.
I SEE...

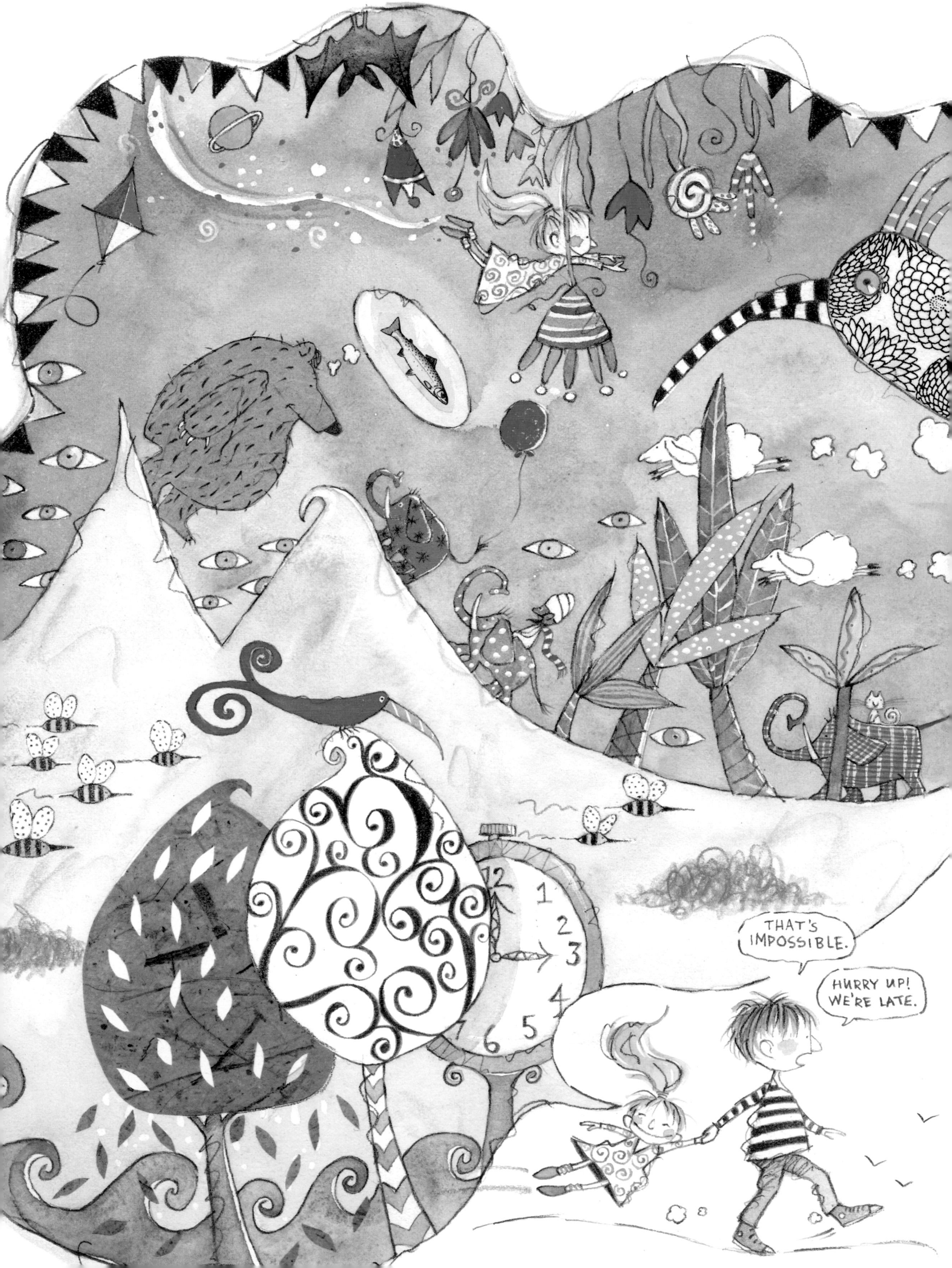
THAT'S IMPOSSIBLE.
HURRY UP! WE'RE LATE.

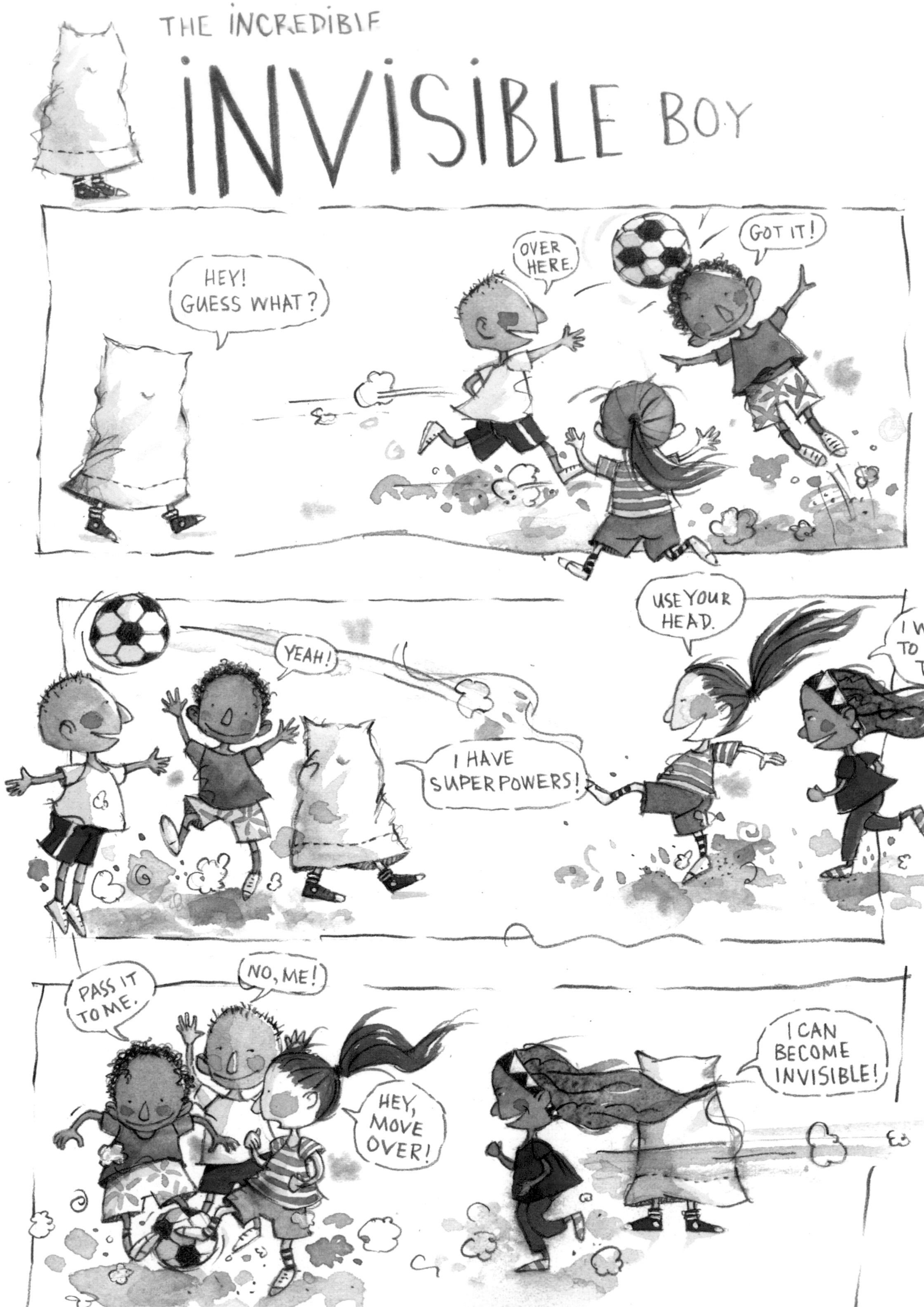
THE INCREDIBLE
INVISIBLE BOY
HEY! GUESS WHAT?
OVER HERE.
GOT IT!
YEAH!
I HAVE SUPERPOWERS!
USE YOUR HEAD.
I WANT TO PLAY TOO.
PASS IT TO ME.
NO, ME!
HEY, MOVE OVER!
I CAN BECOME INVISIBLE!

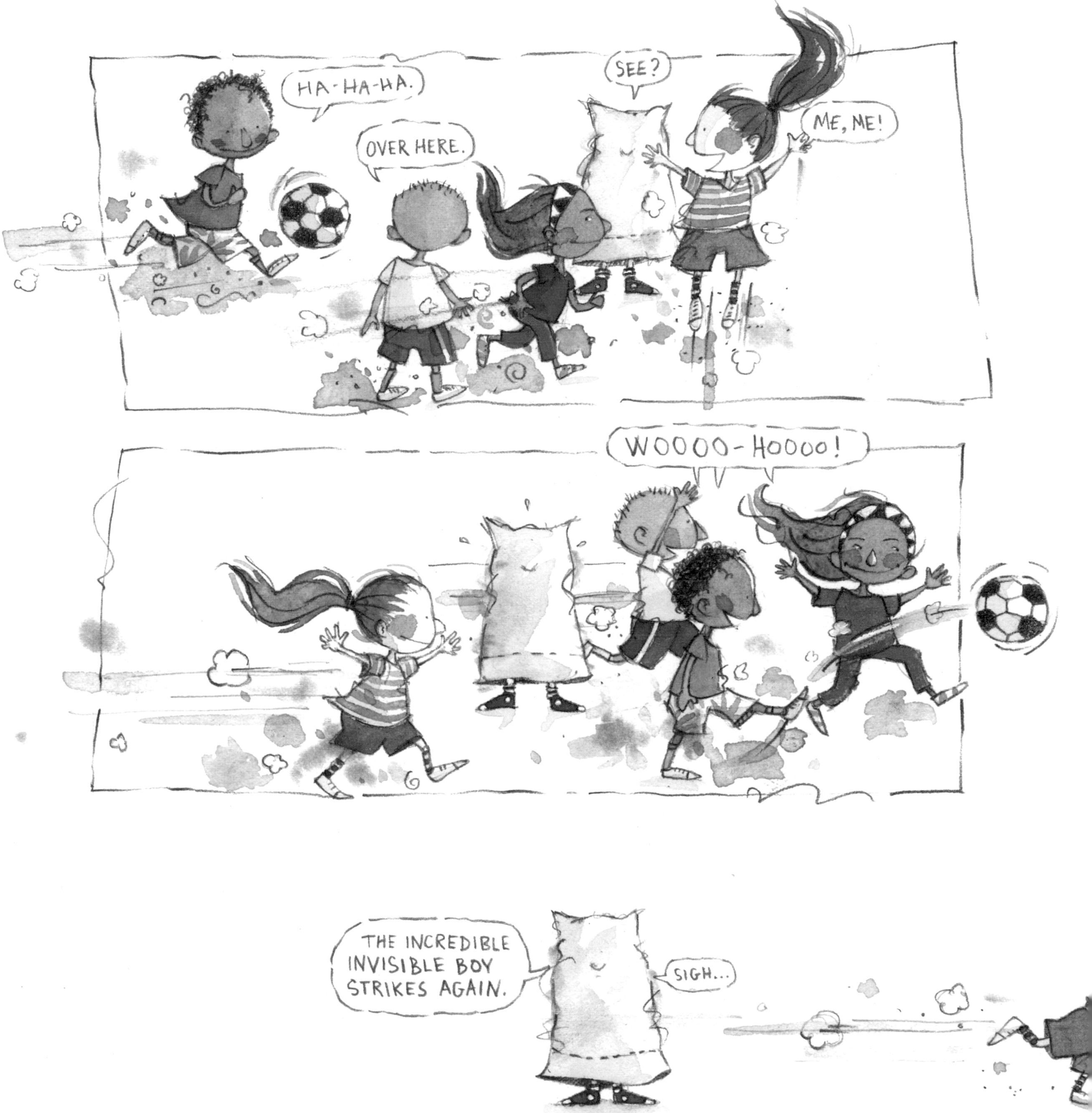
HA-HA-HA.
OVER HERE.
SEE?
ME, ME!
WOOOO-HOOOO!
THE INCREDIBLE INVISIBLE BOY STRIKES AGAIN.
SIGH...

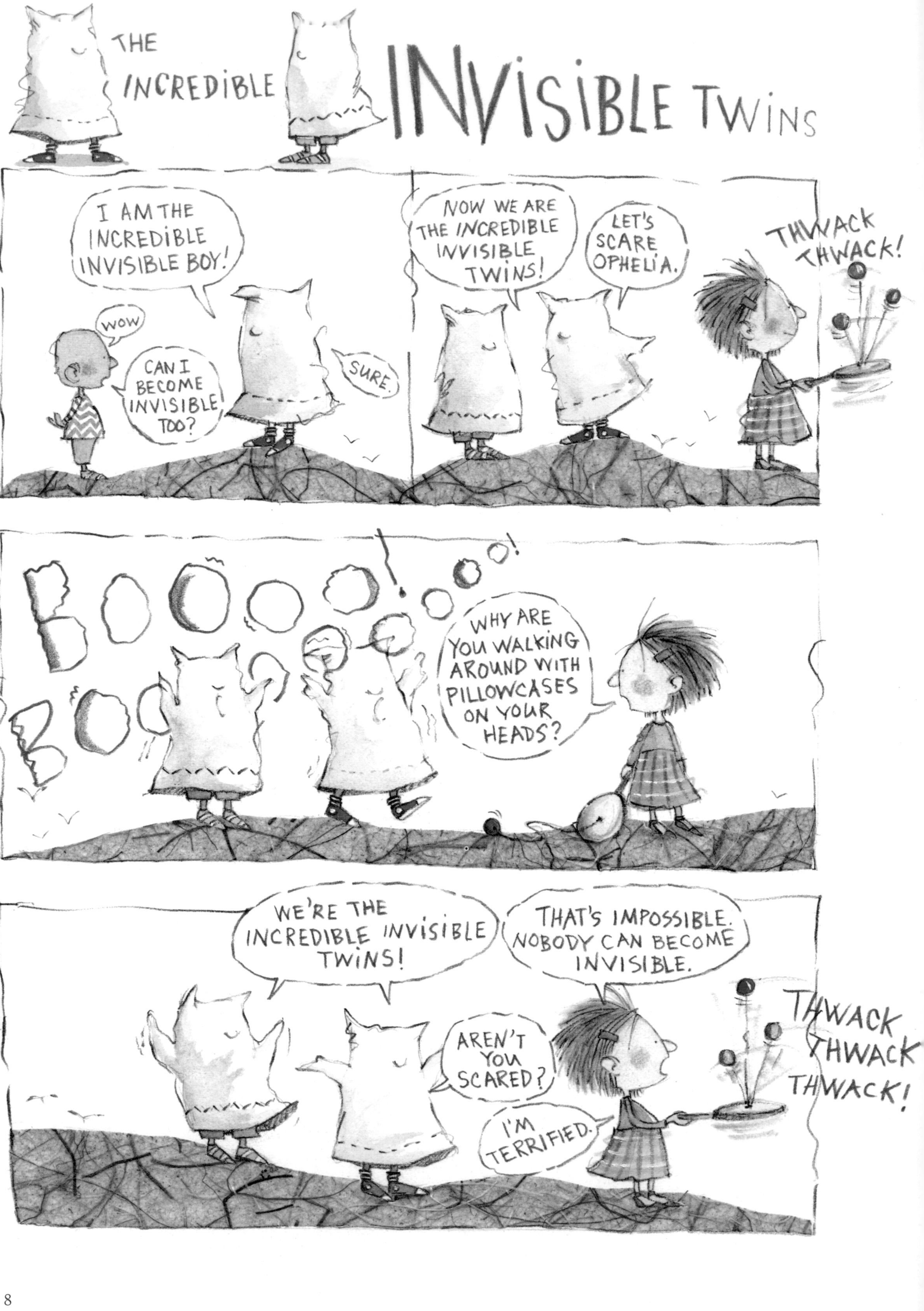
THE INCREDIBLE INVISIBLE TWINS
I AM THE INCREDIBLE INVISIBLE BOY!
WOW
CAN I BECOME INVISIBLE TOO?
SURE.
NOW WE ARE THE INCREDIBLE INVISIBLE TWINS!
LET'S SCARE OPHELIA.
THWACK THWACK!
BOOOO!OOOO!
BOO
WHY ARE YOU WALKING AROUND WITH PILLOWCASES ON YOUR HEADS?
WE'RE THE INCREDIBLE INVISIBLE TWINS!
THAT'S IMPOSSIBLE. NOBODY CAN BECOME INVISIBLE.
AREN'T YOU SCARED?
I'M TERRIFIED.
THWACK THWACK THWACK!

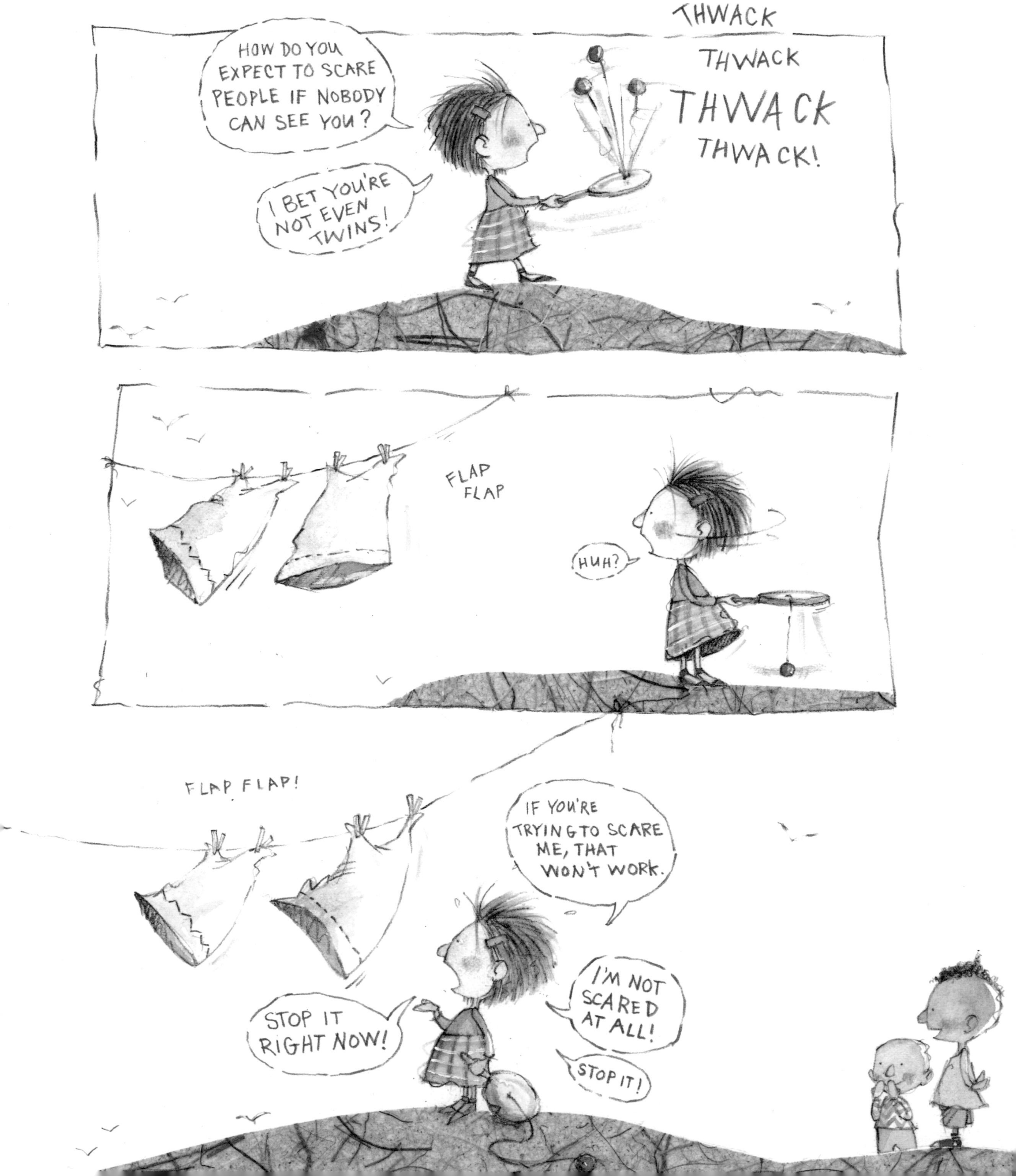
HOW DO YOU EXPECT TO SCARE PEOPLE IF NOBODY CAN SEE YOU?
I BET YOU'RE NOT EVEN TWINS!
THWACK
THWACK
THWACK
THWACK!
FLAP FLAP
HUH?
FLAP FLAP!
IF YOU'RE TRYING TO SCARE ME, THAT WON'T WORK.
I'M NOT SCARED AT ALL!
STOP IT RIGHT NOW!
STOP IT!

WHO? ME?

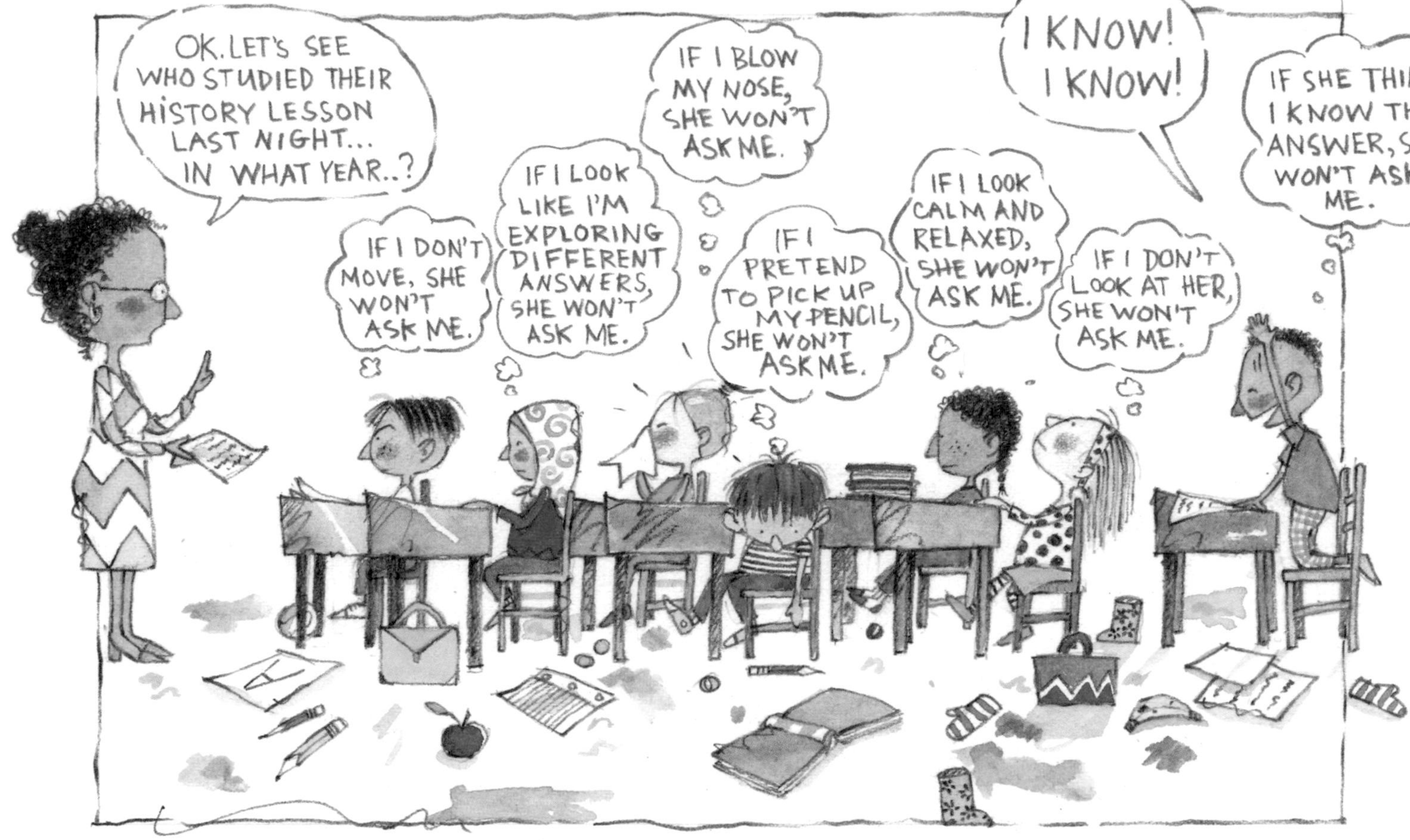
OK. LET'S SEE WHO STUDIED THEIR HISTORY LESSON LAST NIGHT... IN WHAT YEAR..?
IF I DON'T MOVE, SHE WON'T ASK ME.
IF I LOOK LIKE I'M EXPLORING DIFFERENT ANSWERS, SHE WON'T ASK ME.
IF I BLOW MY NOSE, SHE WON'T ASK ME.
IF I PRETEND TO PICK UP MY PENCIL, SHE WON'T ASK ME.
IF I LOOK CALM AND RELAXED, SHE WON'T ASK ME.
IF I DON'T LOOK AT HER, SHE WON'T ASK ME.
I KNOW! I KNOW!
IF SHE THINKS I KNOW THE ANSWER, SHE WON'T ASK ME.

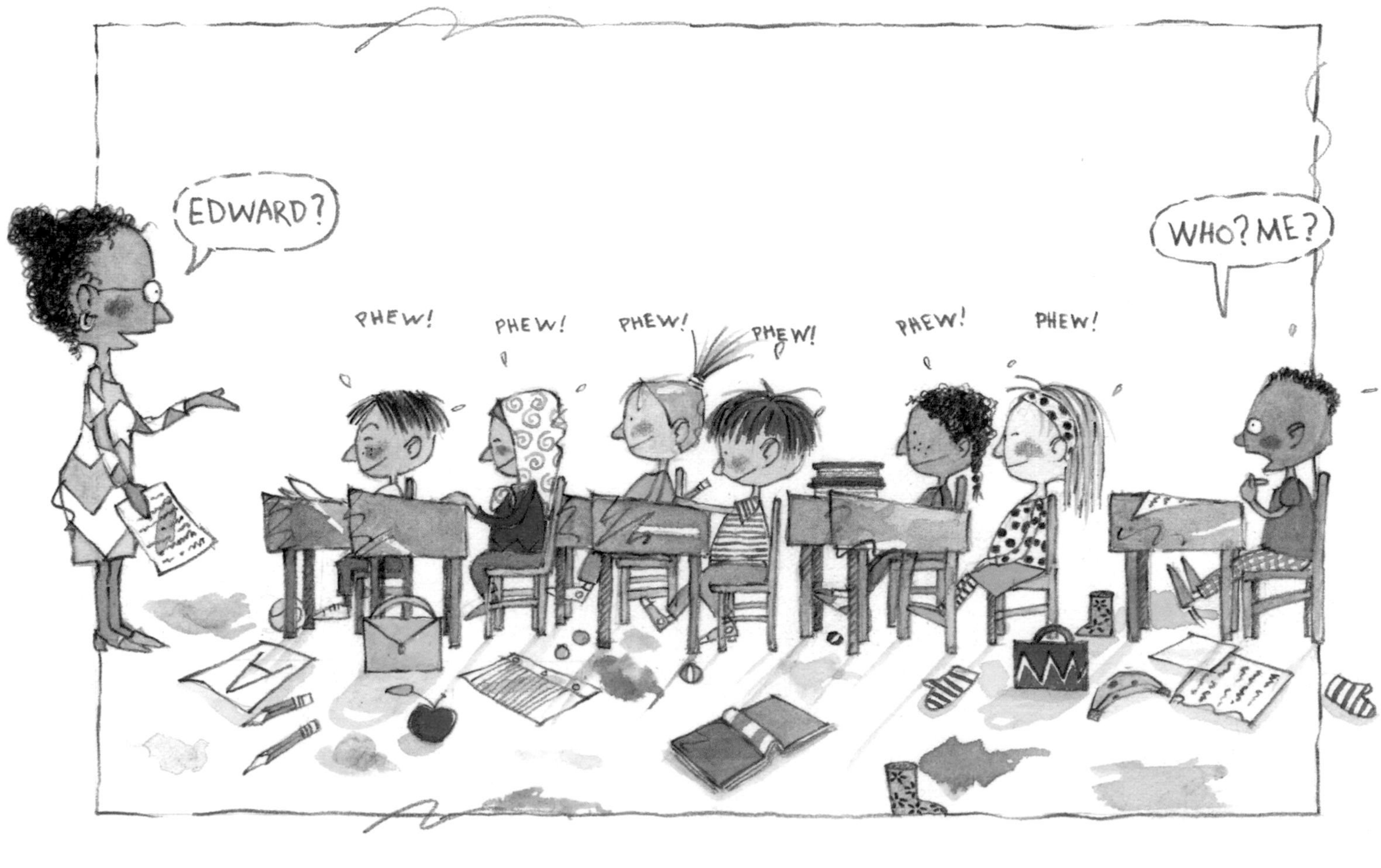
EDWARD?
PHEW!
PHEW!
PHEW!
PHEW!
PHEW!
PHEW!
WHO? ME?

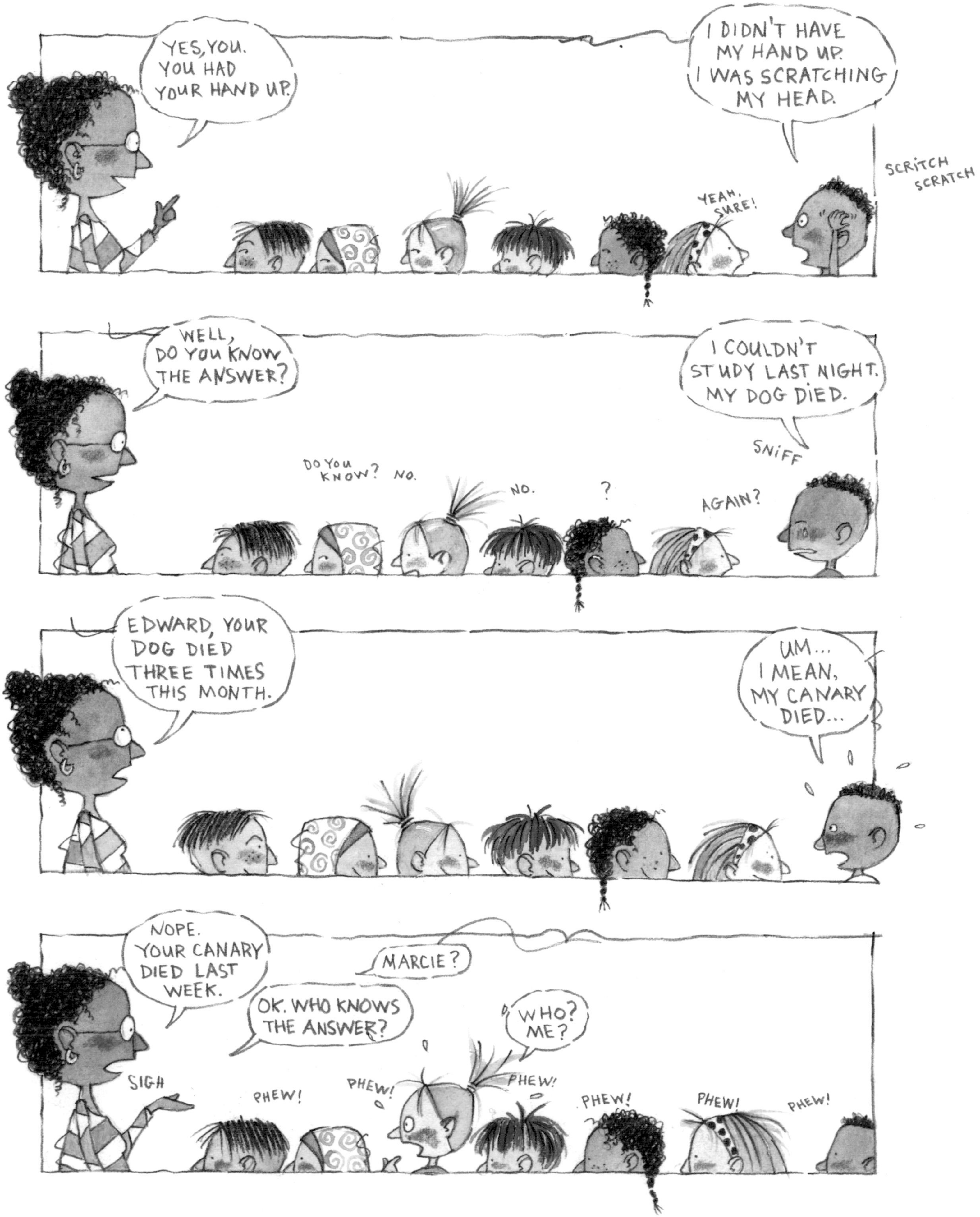
YES, YOU. YOU HAD YOUR HAND UP.
I DIDN'T HAVE MY HAND UP. I WAS SCRATCHING MY HEAD.
YEAH, SURE!
SCRITCH SCRATCH
WELL, DO YOU KNOW THE ANSWER?
I COULDN'T STUDY LAST NIGHT. MY DOG DIED.
SNIFF
DO YOU KNOW? NO.
NO.
?
AGAIN?
EDWARD, YOUR DOG DIED THREE TIMES THIS MONTH.
UM... I MEAN, MY CANARY DIED...
NOPE. YOUR CANARY DIED LAST WEEK.
OK. WHO KNOWS THE ANSWER?
MARCIE?
WHO? ME?
SIGH
PHEW!
PHEW!
PHEW!
PHEW!
PHEW!
PHEW!

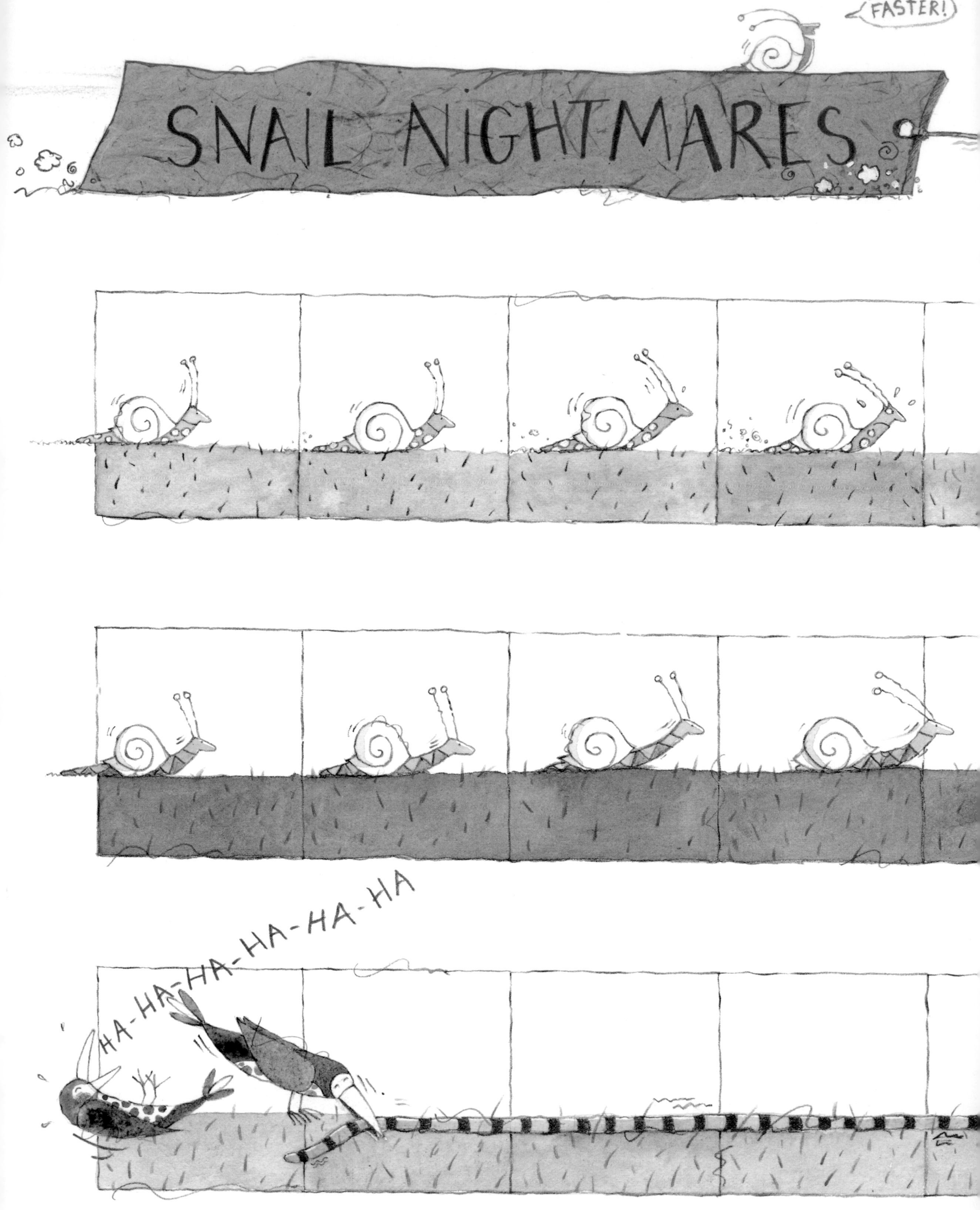
FASTER!
SNAIL NIGHTMARES
HA-HA-HA-HA-HA-HA-HA

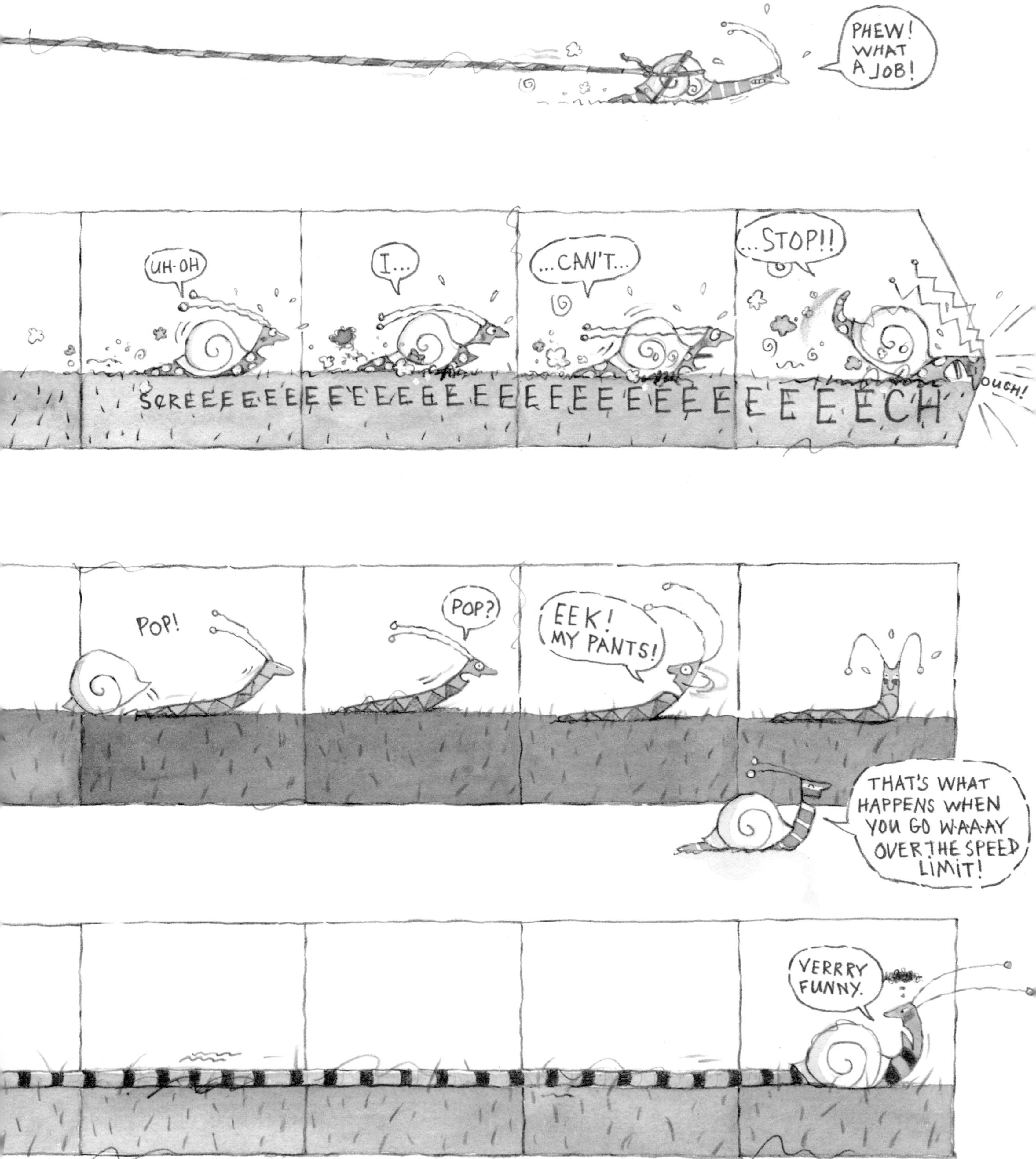
PHEW! WHAT A JOB!
UH-OH
I...
...CAN'T...
...STOP!!
SCREEEEEEEEEEEEEEEEEEEEEEEEEEEEEEECH
OUCH!
POP!
POP?
EEK! MY PANTS!
THAT'S WHAT HAPPENS WHEN YOU GO W-A-A-AY OVER THE SPEED LIMIT!
VERRRY FUNNY.

WHAT DO CATS SEE?

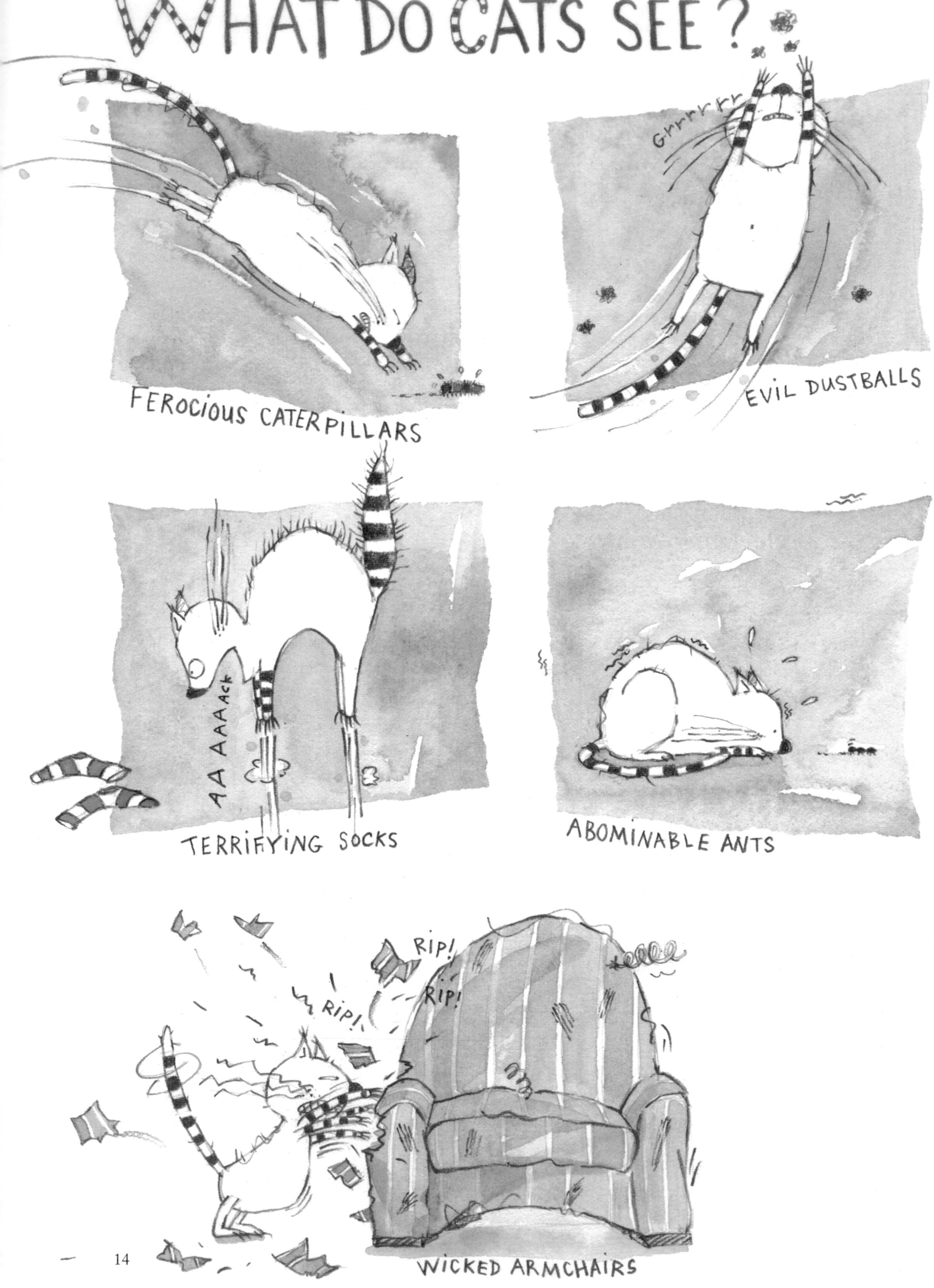
Grrrrrr
AAAAAAck
Rip!
Rip!
Rip!

FEROCIOUS CATERPILLARS

EVIL DUSTBALLS

TERRIFYING SOCKS

ABOMINABLE ANTS

WICKED ARMCHAIRS

WHAT GAMES DO CATS PLAY?

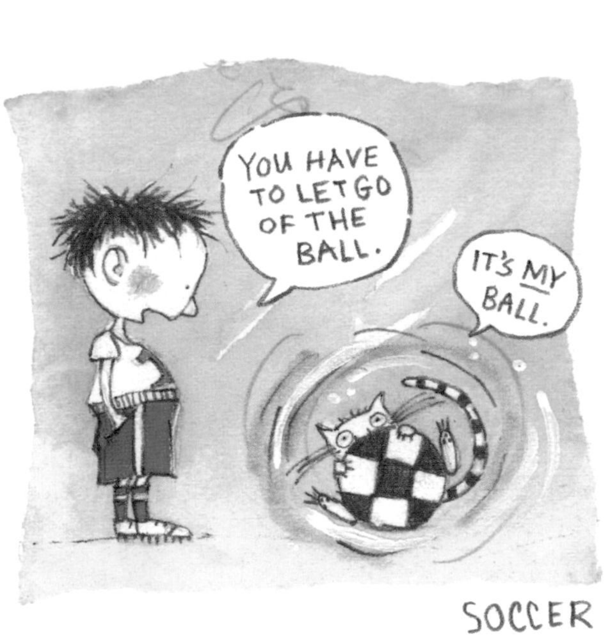
YOU HAVE TO LET GO OF THE BALL.
IT'S MY BALL.

SOCCER

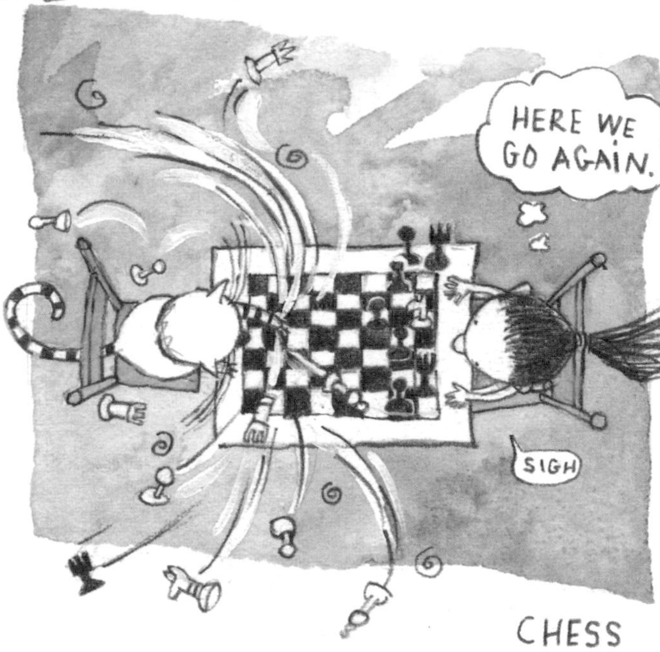
HERE WE GO AGAIN.
SIGH

CHESS

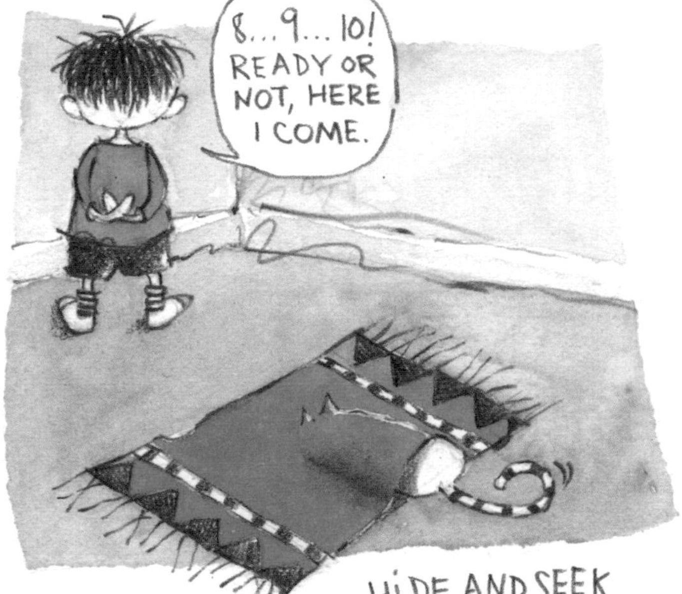
8... 9... 10! READY OR NOT, HERE I COME.

HIDE AND SEEK

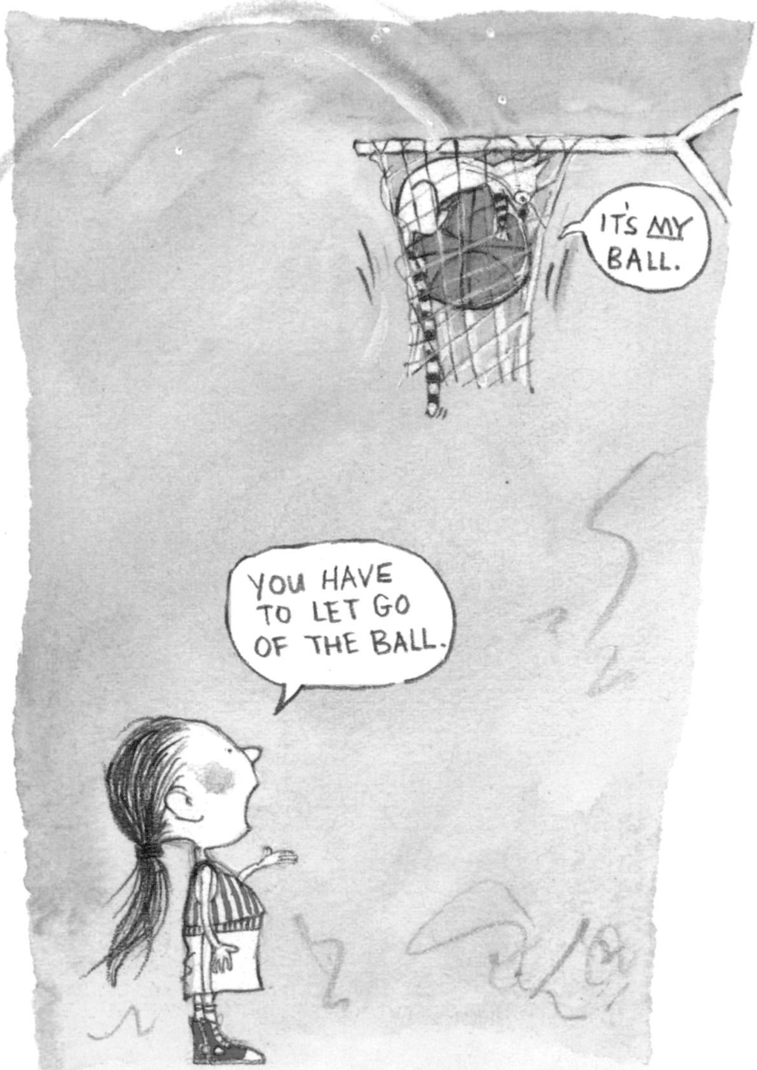
IT'S MY BALL.
YOU HAVE TO LET GO OF THE BALL.

BASKETBALL

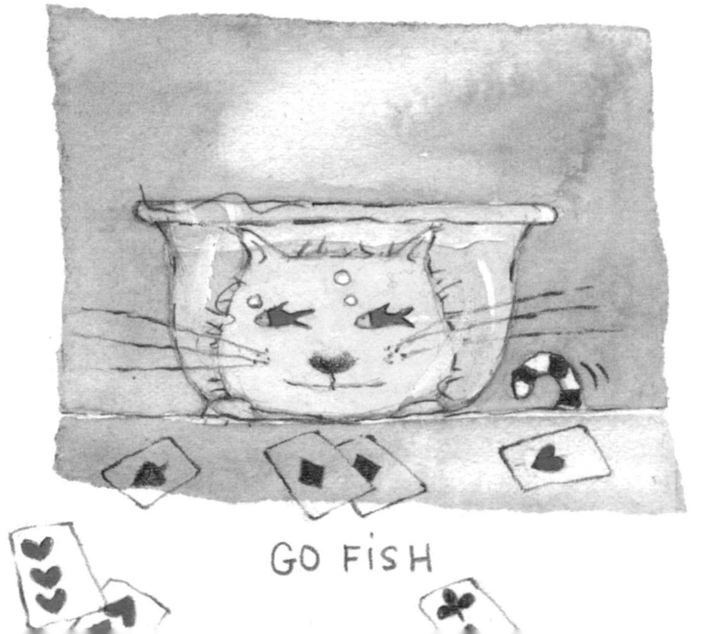

GO FISH

NOBODY NOSE

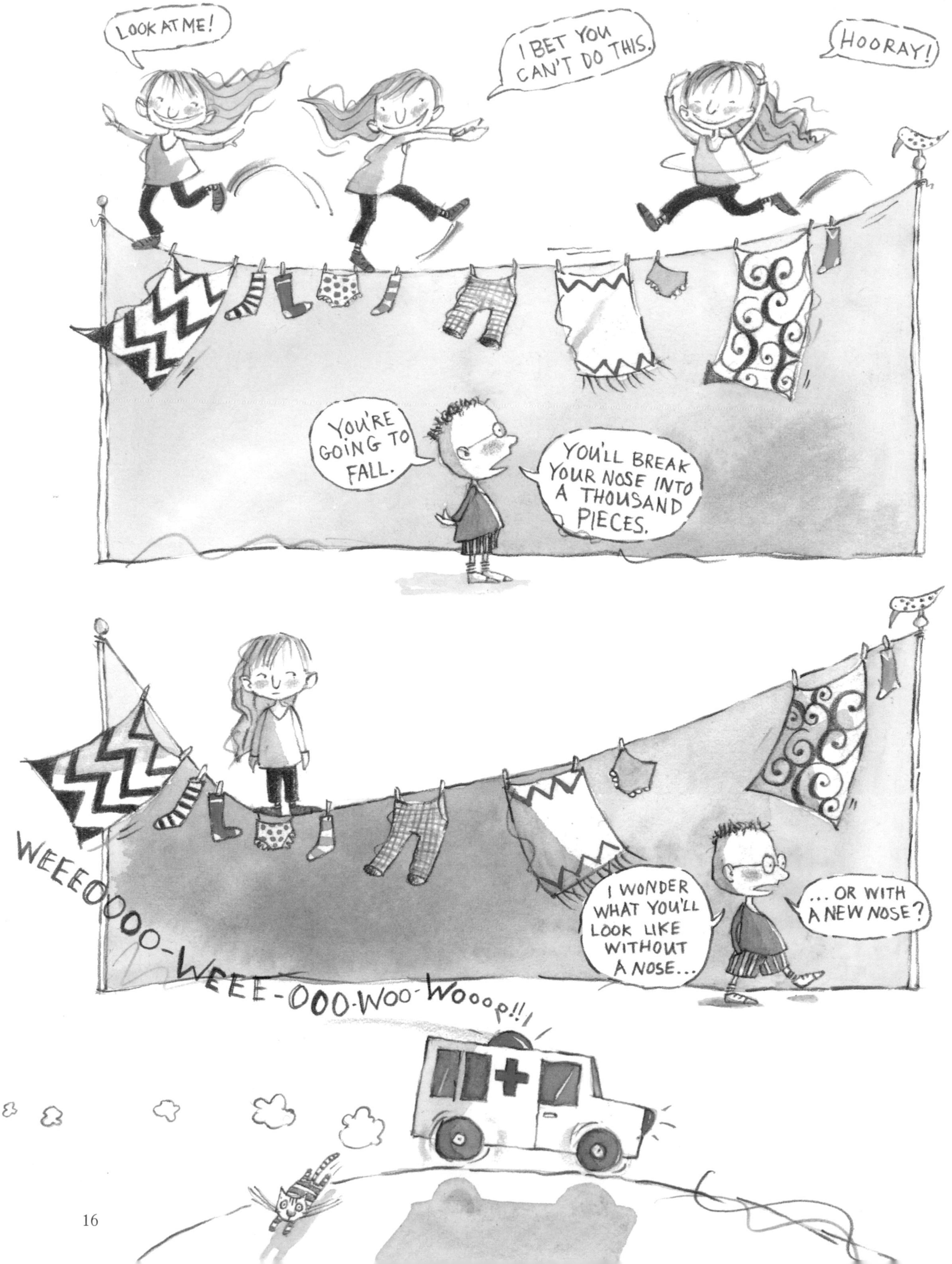
LOOK AT ME!
I BET YOU CAN'T DO THIS.
HOORAY!
YOU'RE GOING TO FALL.
YOU'LL BREAK YOUR NOSE INTO A THOUSAND PIECES.
I WONDER WHAT YOU'LL LOOK LIKE WITHOUT A NOSE...
...OR WITH A NEW NOSE?
WEEEOOOO-WEEE-OOO-WOO-WOOOP!!!

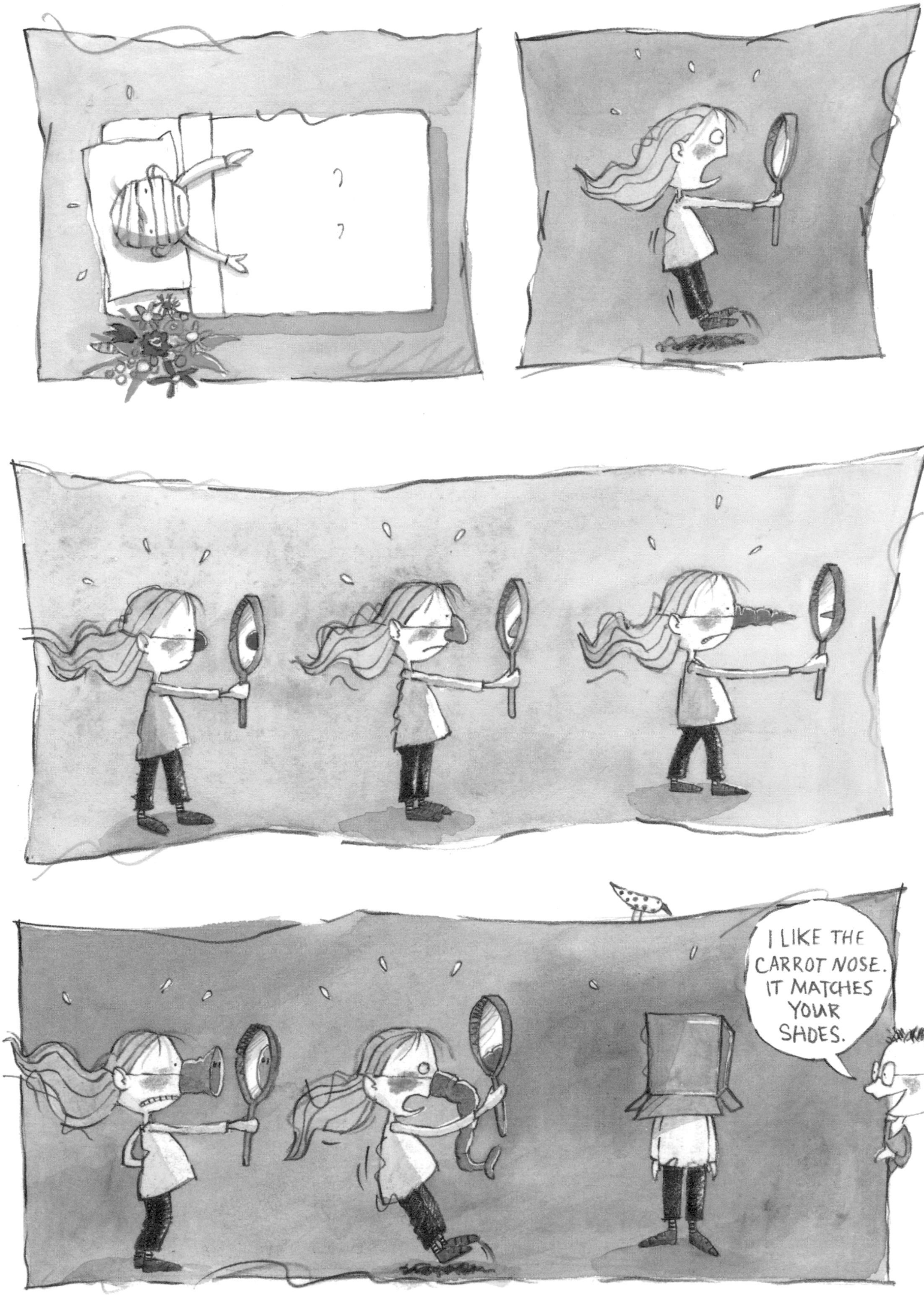
I LIKE THE CARROT NOSE. IT MATCHES YOUR SHOES.

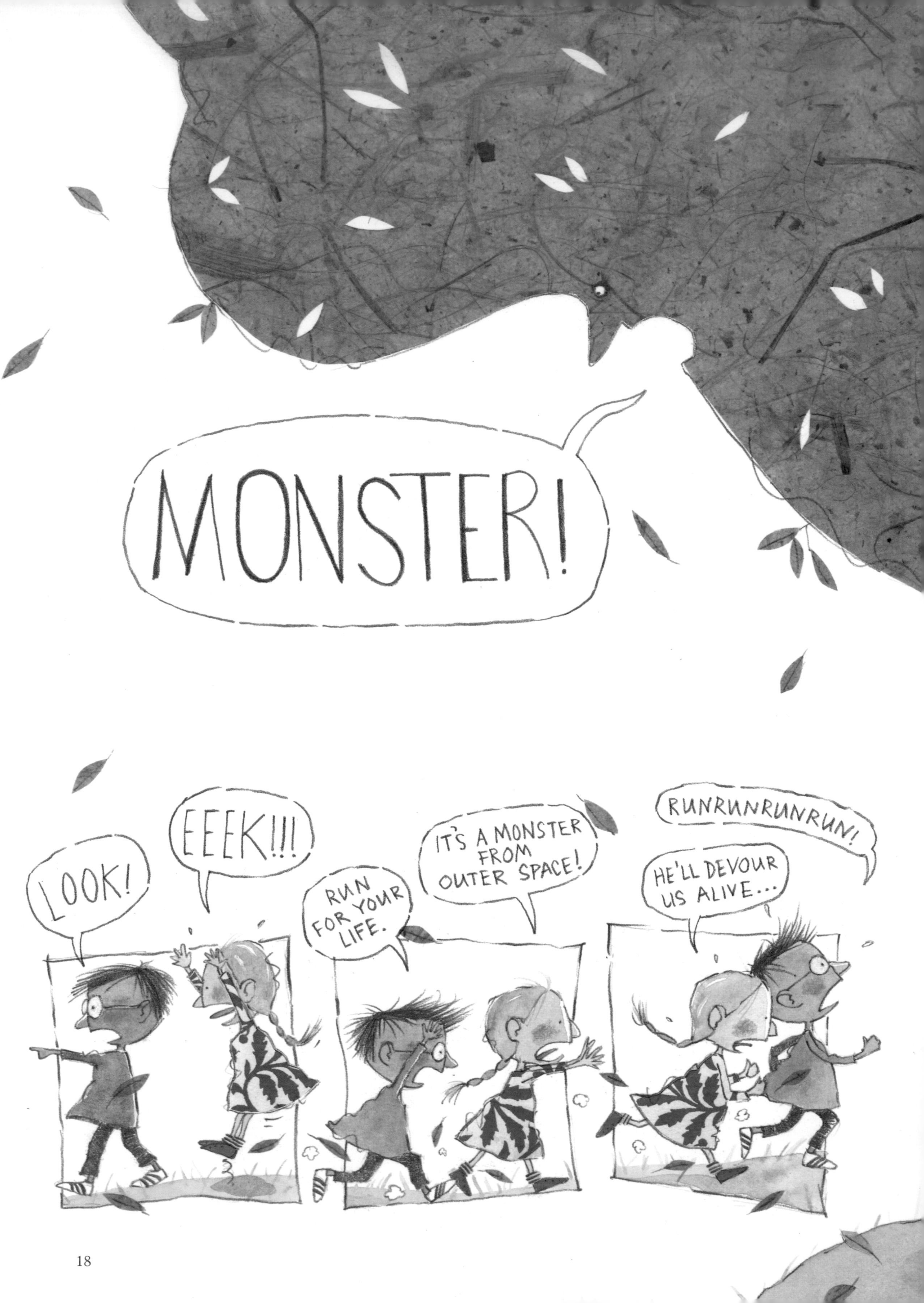
MONSTER!
LOOK!
EEEK!!!
RUN FOR YOUR LIFE.
IT'S A MONSTER FROM OUTER SPACE!
RUNRUNRUNRUN!
HE'LL DEVOUR US ALIVE...

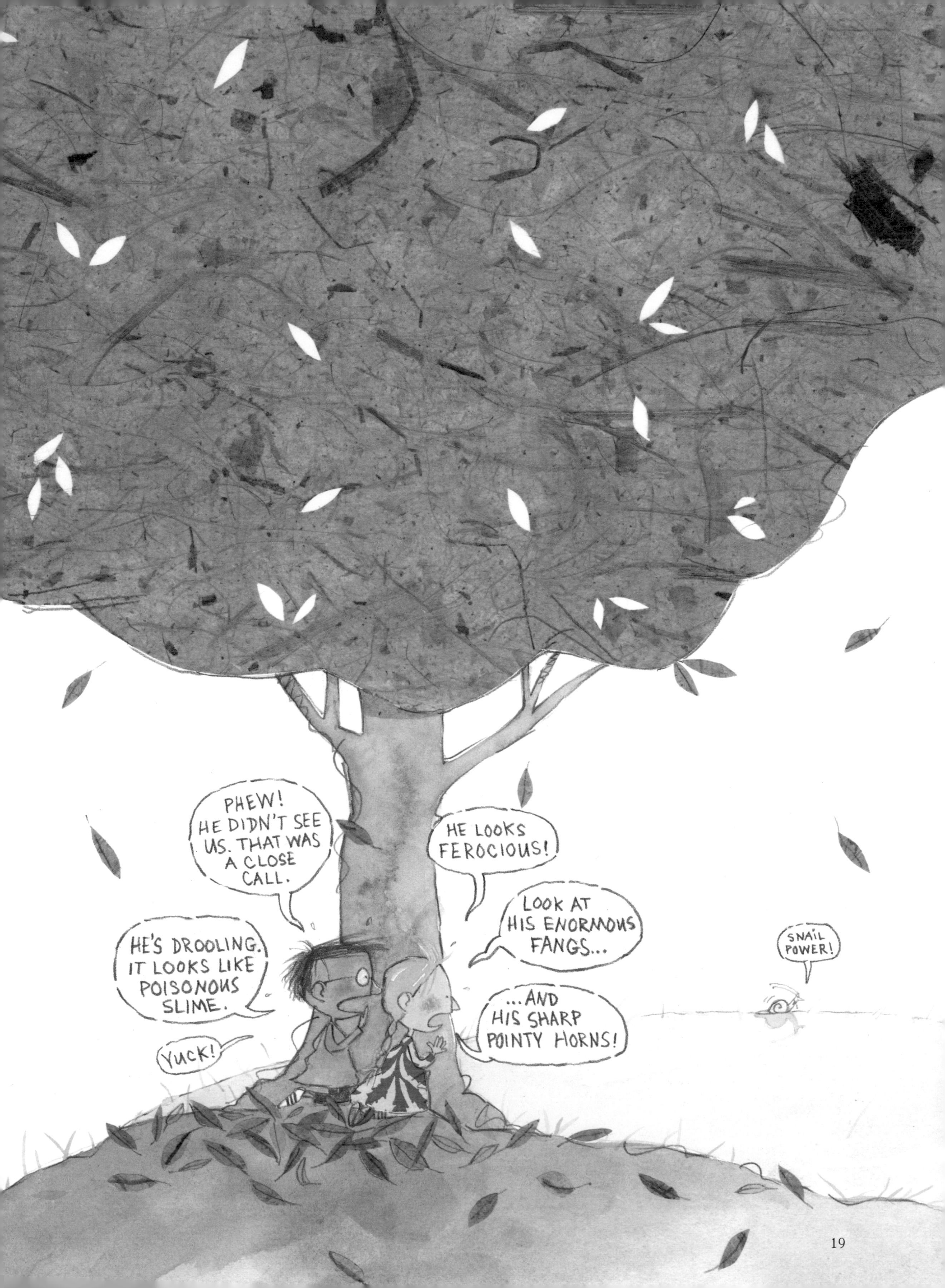
PHEW! HE DIDN'T SEE US. THAT WAS A CLOSE CALL.
HE LOOKS FEROCIOUS!
LOOK AT HIS ENORMOUS FANGS...
HE'S DROOLING. IT LOOKS LIKE POISONOUS SLIME.
...AND HIS SHARP POINTY HORNS!
YUCK!
SNAIL POWER!

JUMP!

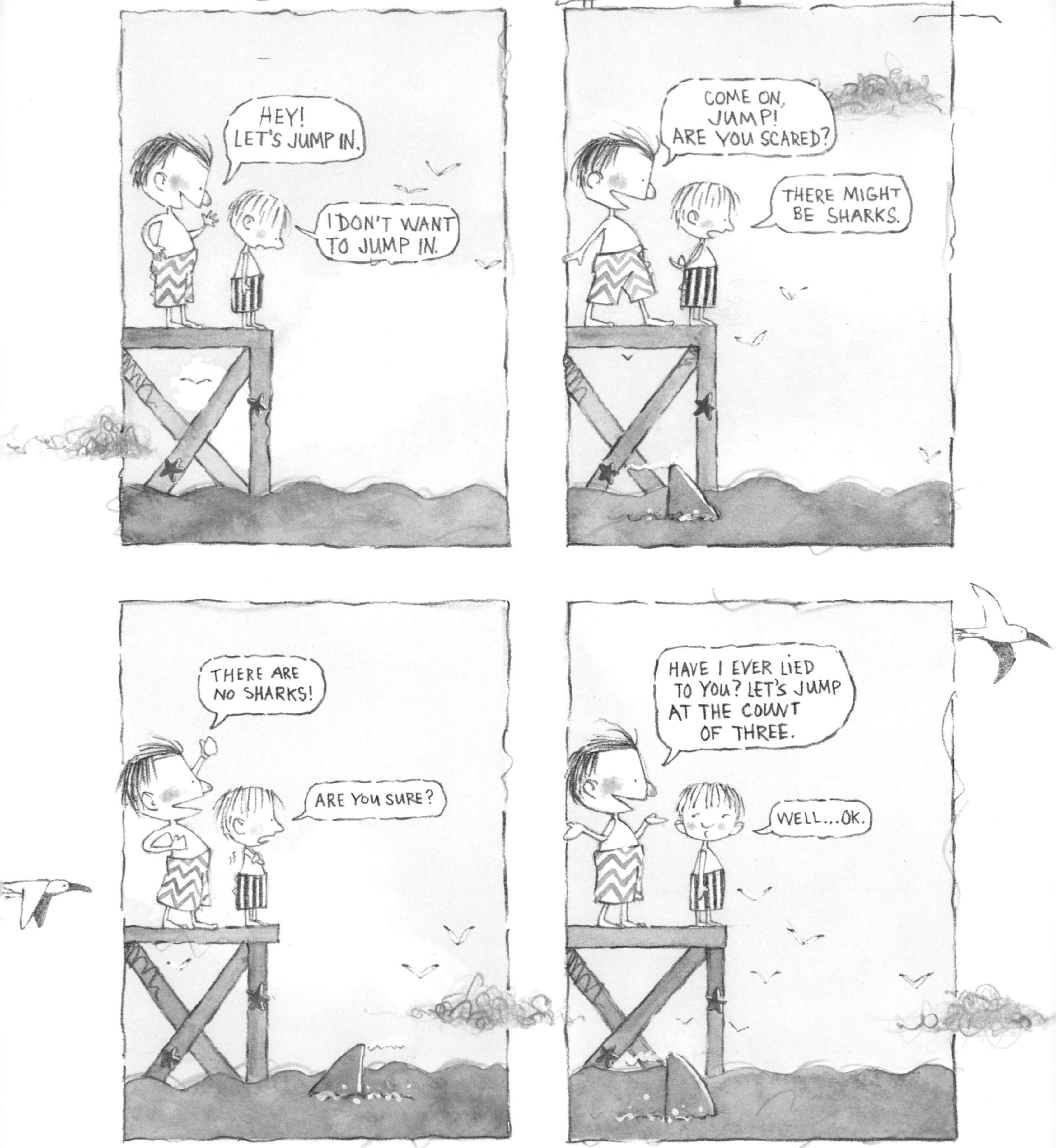
HEY! LET'S JUMP IN.
I DON'T WANT TO JUMP IN.
COME ON, JUMP! ARE YOU SCARED?
THERE MIGHT BE SHARKS.
THERE ARE NO SHARKS!
ARE YOU SURE?
HAVE I EVER LIED TO YOU? LET'S JUMP AT THE COUNT OF THREE.
WELL...OK.

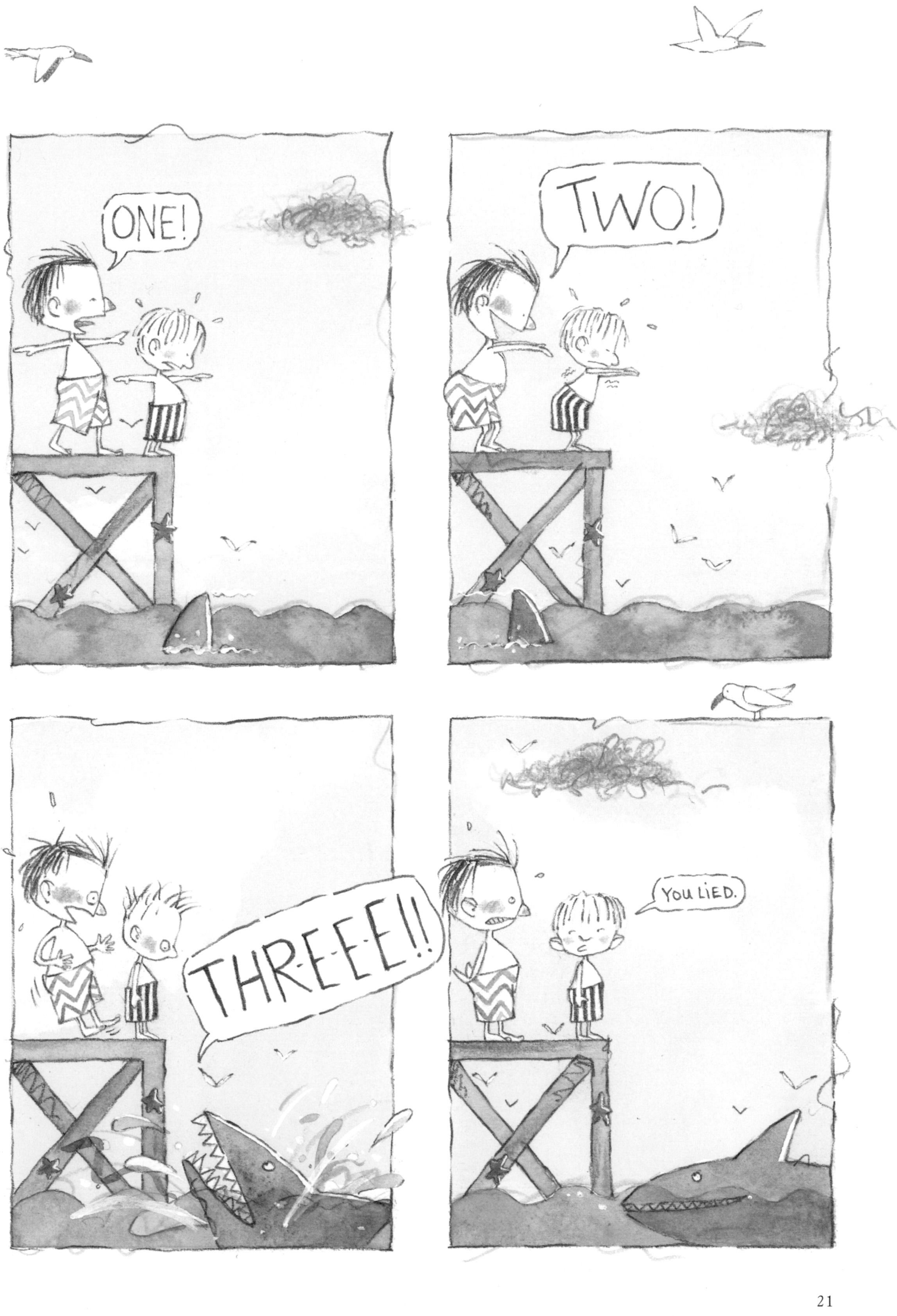
ONE!
TWO!
THR-E-E-E!!
YOU LIED.

WORMS

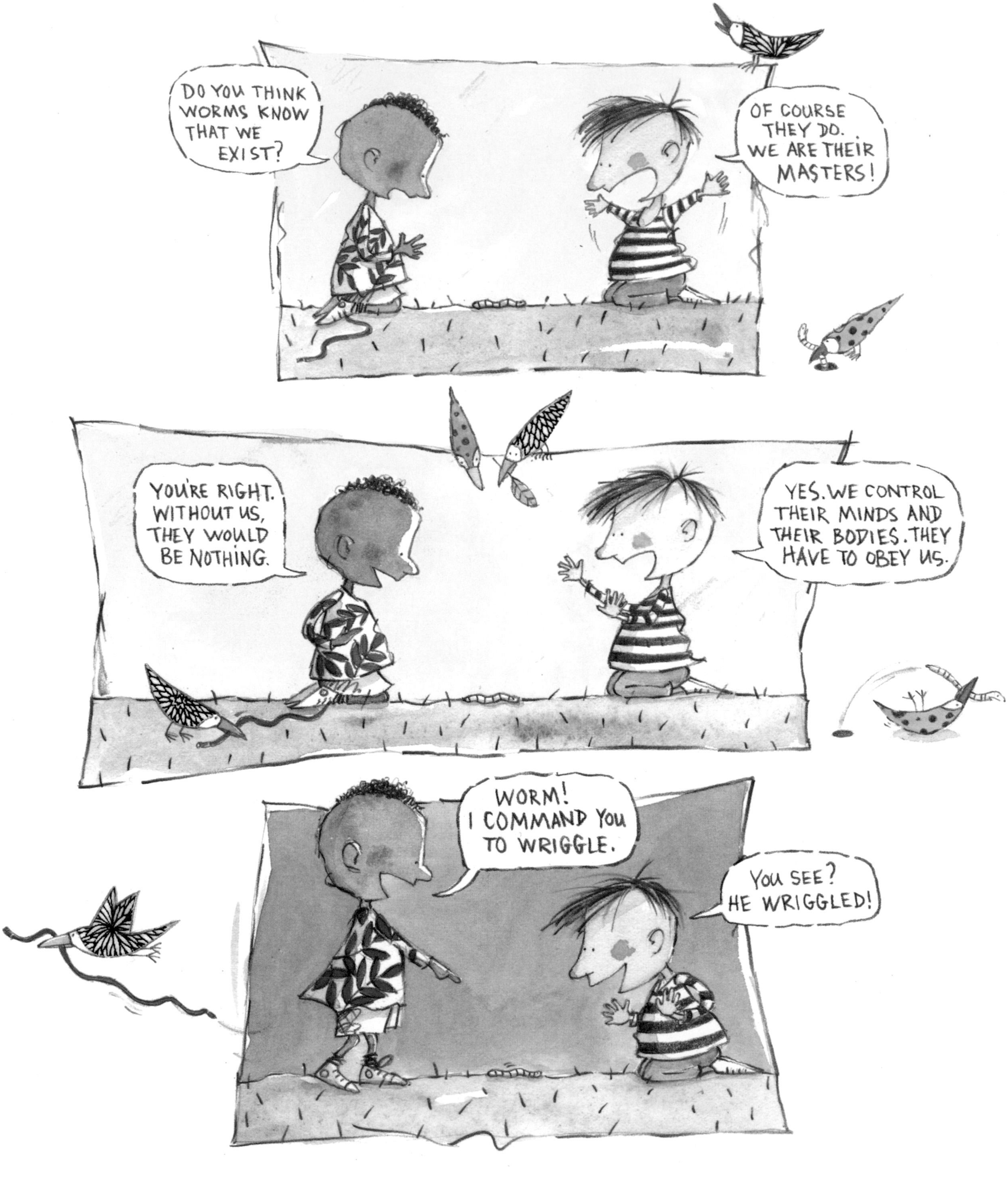
DO YOU THINK WORMS KNOW THAT WE EXIST?
OF COURSE THEY DO. WE ARE THEIR MASTERS!
YOU'RE RIGHT. WITHOUT US, THEY WOULD BE NOTHING.
YES. WE CONTROL THEIR MINDS AND THEIR BODIES. THEY HAVE TO OBEY US.
WORM! I COMMAND YOU TO WRIGGLE.
YOU SEE? HE WRIGGLED!

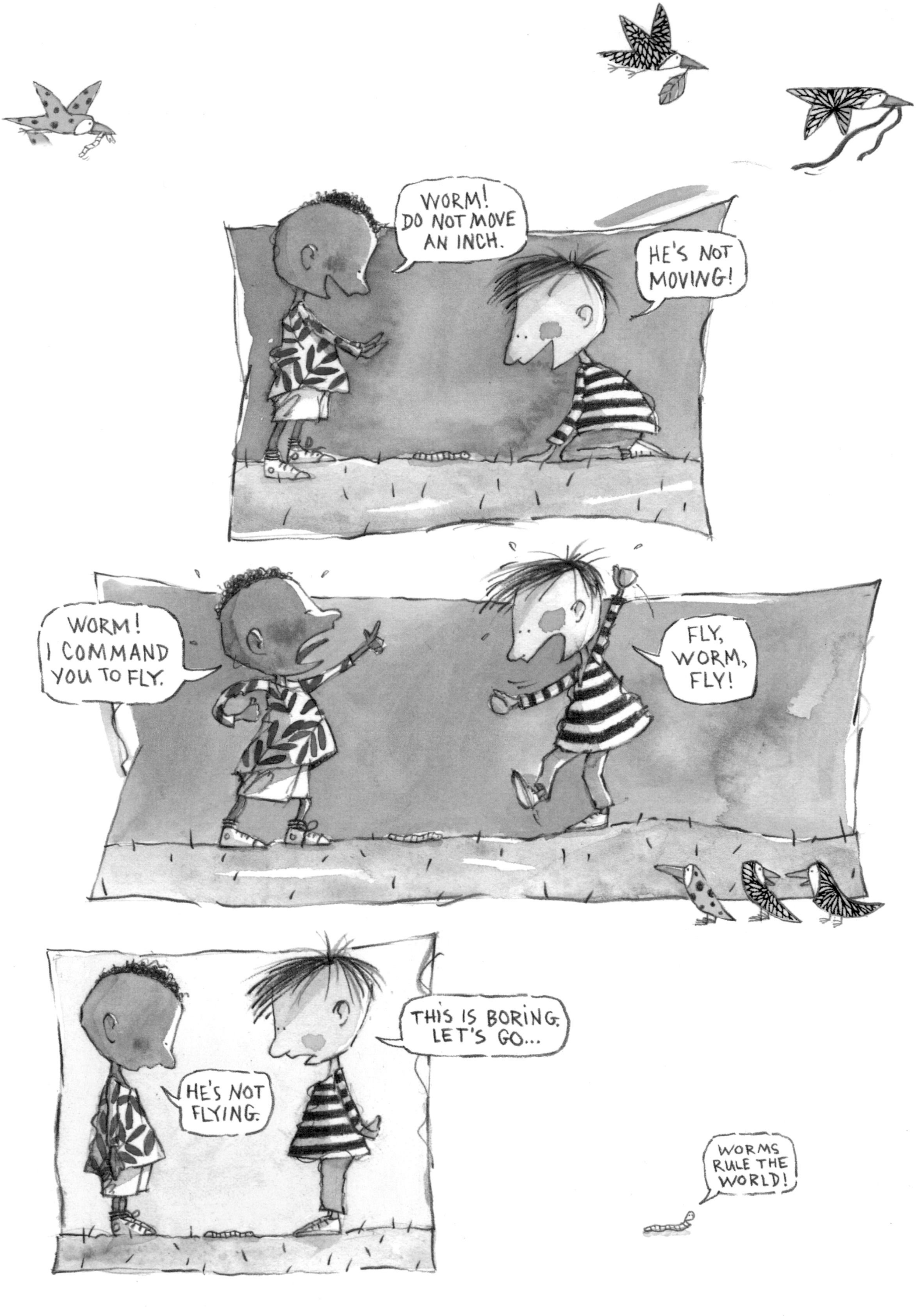
WORM! DO NOT MOVE AN INCH.
HE'S NOT MOVING!
WORM! I COMMAND YOU TO FLY.
FLY, WORM, FLY!
THIS IS BORING. LET'S GO...
HE'S NOT FLYING.
WORMS RULE THE WORLD!

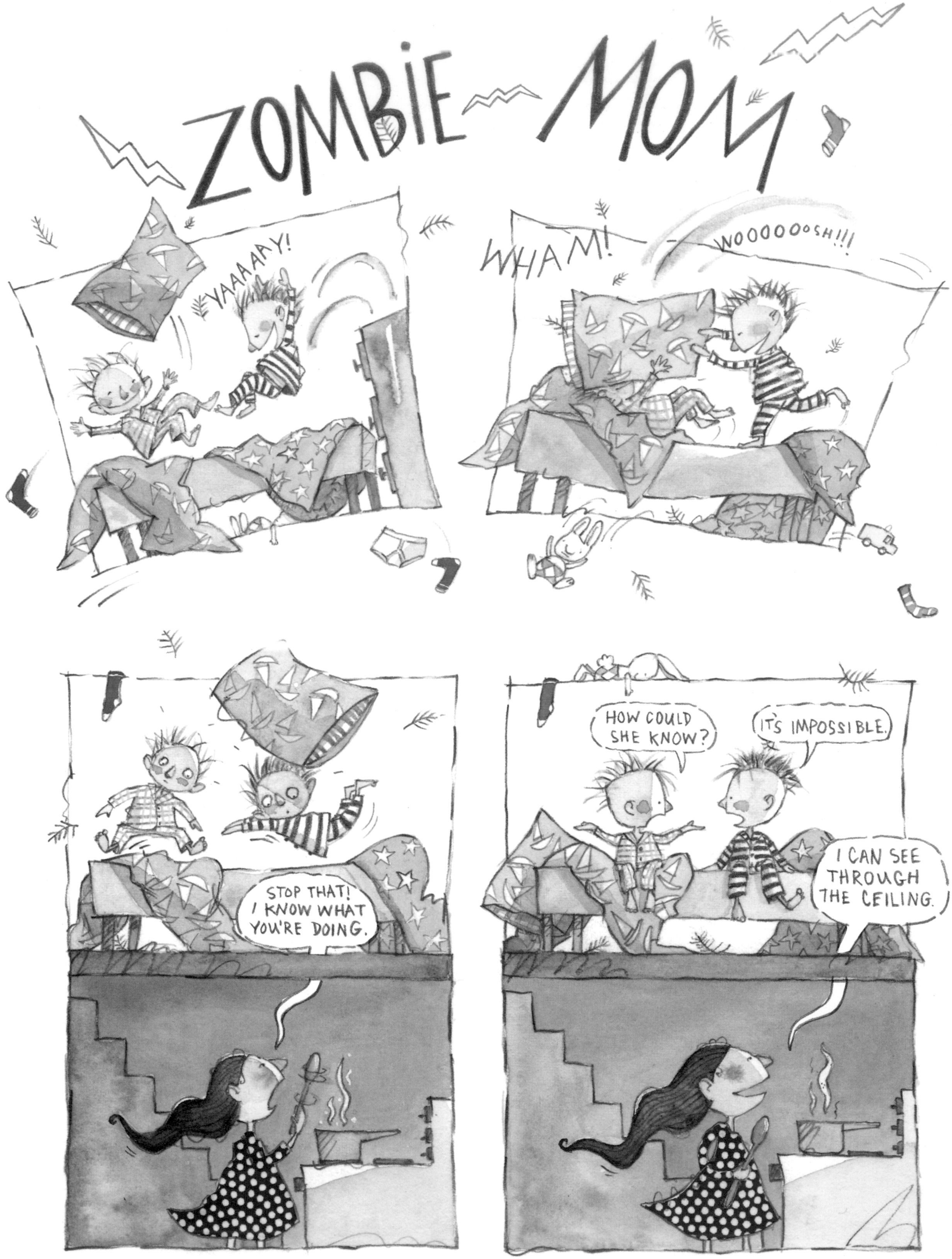
ZOMBIE MOM
YAAAAAY!
WHAM!
WOOOOOOSH!!!
STOP THAT! I KNOW WHAT YOU'RE DOING.
HOW COULD SHE KNOW?
IT'S IMPOSSIBLE.
I CAN SEE THROUGH THE CEILING.

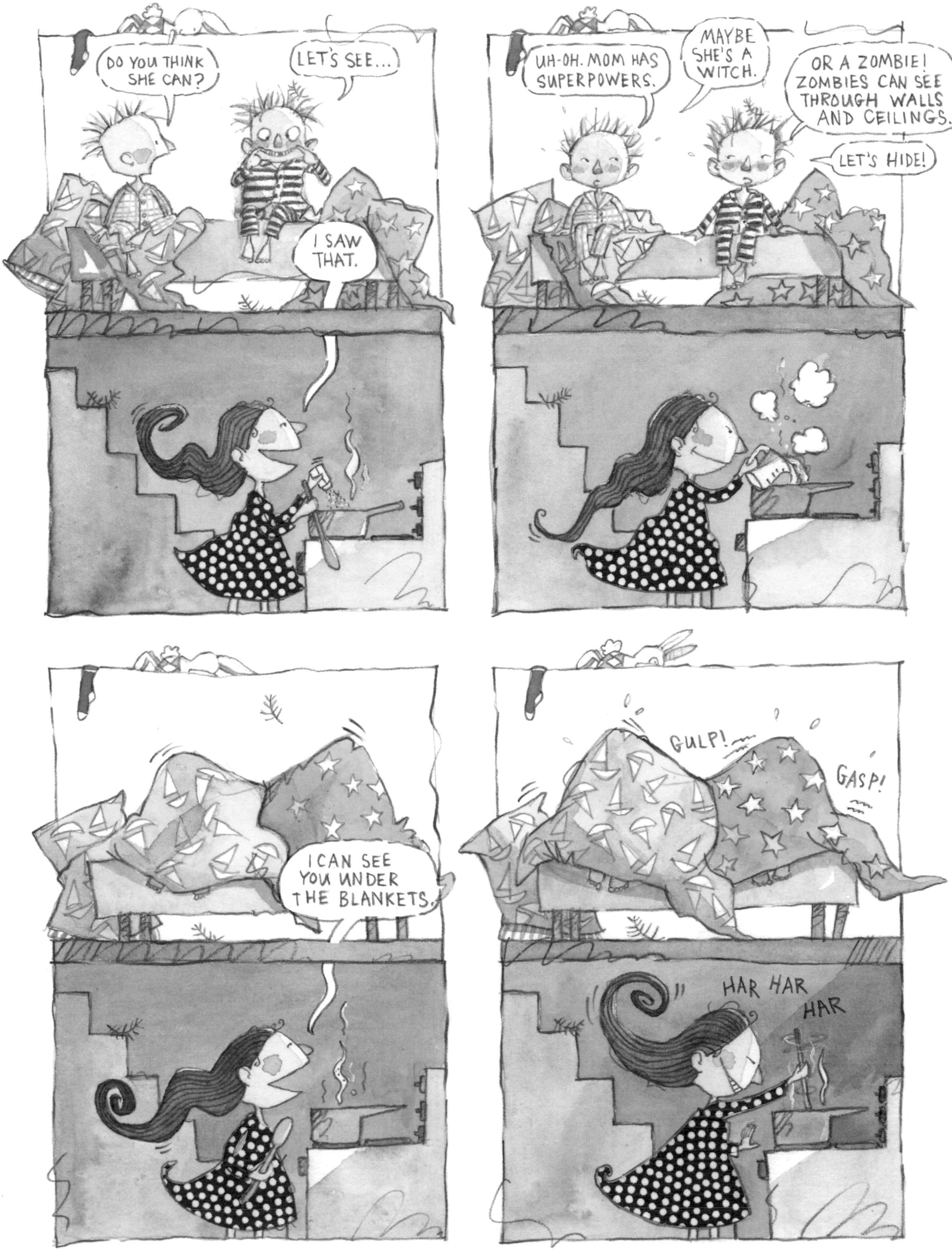
DO YOU THINK SHE CAN?
LET'S SEE...
I SAW THAT.
UH-OH. MOM HAS SUPERPOWERS.
MAYBE SHE'S A WITCH.
OR A ZOMBIE! ZOMBIES CAN SEE THROUGH WALLS AND CEILINGS.
LET'S HIDE!
I CAN SEE YOU UNDER THE BLANKETS.
GULP!
GASP!
HAR HAR HAR

THE SECRET LIFE OF SNAILS

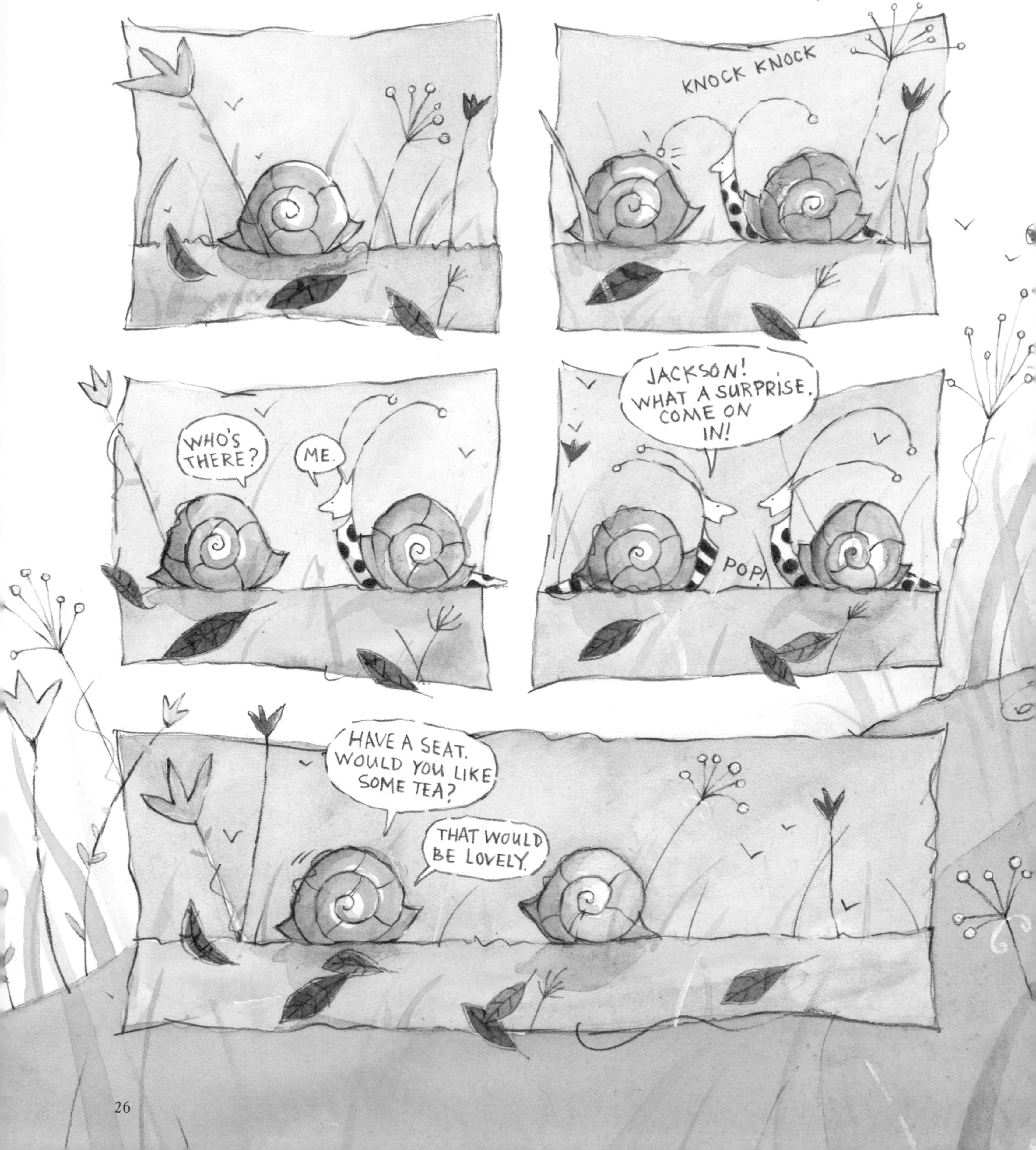
KNOCK KNOCK
WHO'S THERE?
ME.
JACKSON! WHAT A SURPRISE. COME ON IN!
POP!
HAVE A SEAT. WOULD YOU LIKE SOME TEA?
THAT WOULD BE LOVELY.

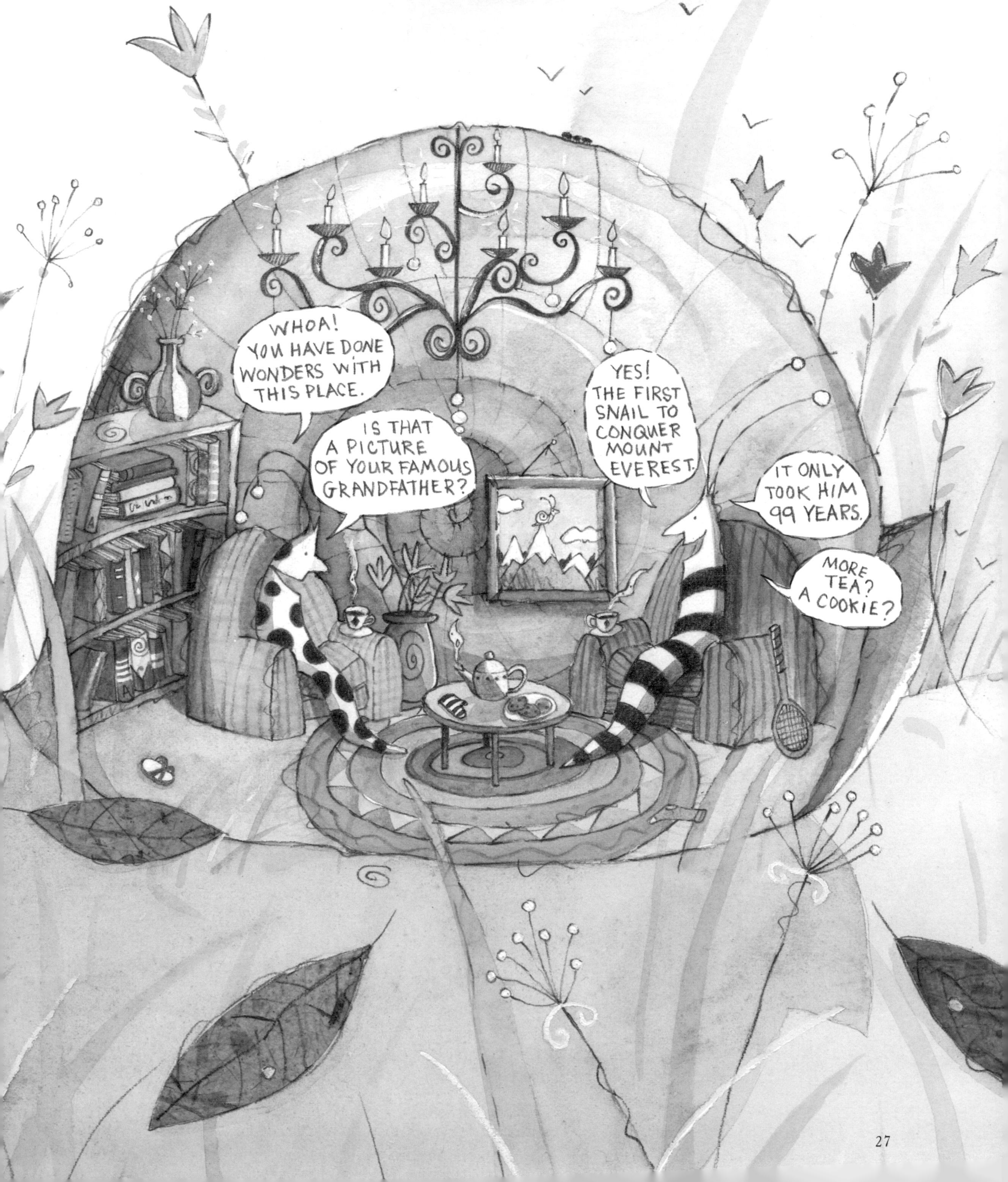
WHOA! YOU HAVE DONE WONDERS WITH THIS PLACE.
IS THAT A PICTURE OF YOUR FAMOUS GRANDFATHER?
YES! THE FIRST SNAIL TO CONQUER MOUNT EVEREST.
IT ONLY TOOK HIM 99 YEARS.
MORE TEA? A COOKIE?

RHISONOROS

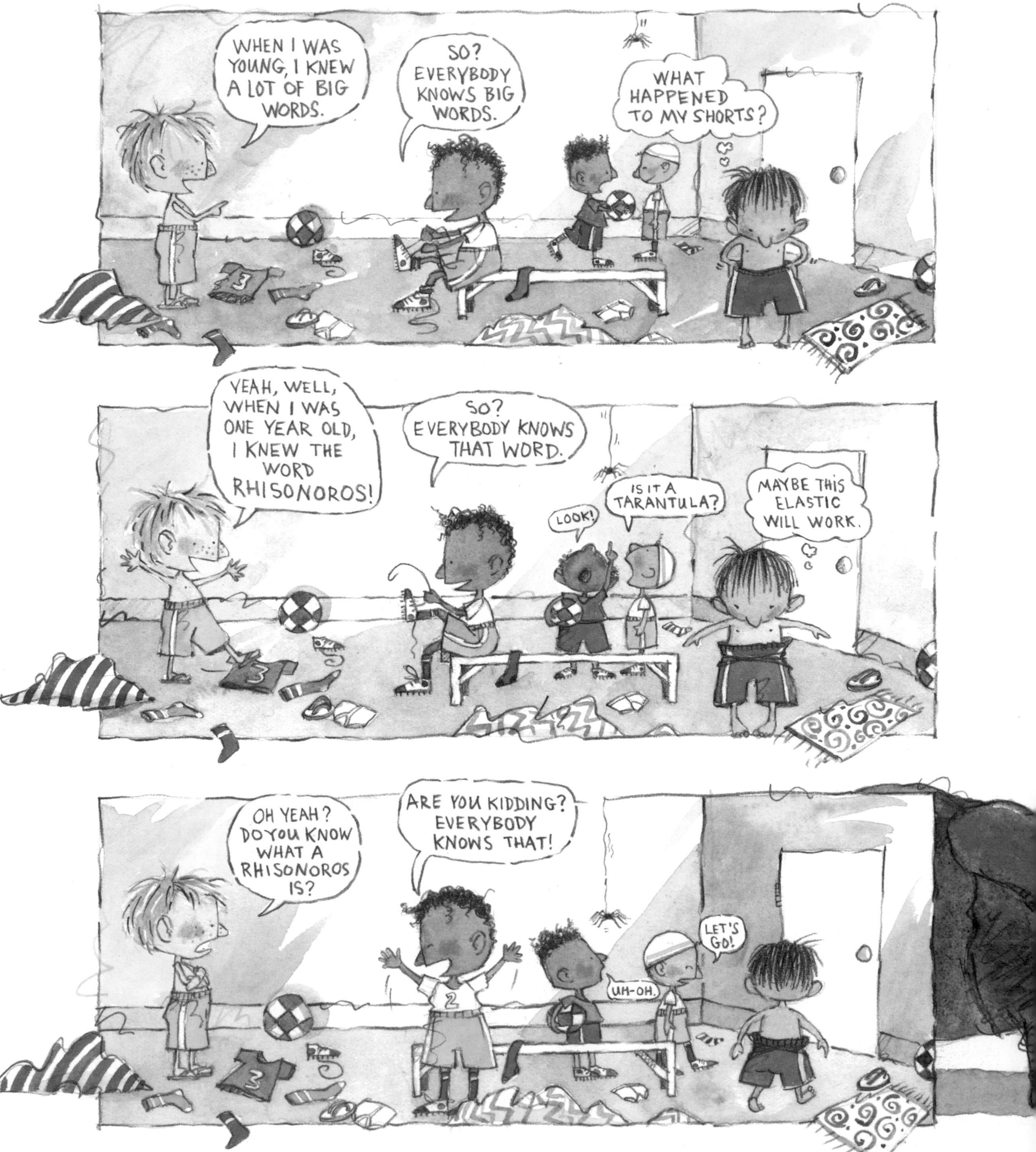
WHEN I WAS YOUNG, I KNEW A LOT OF BIG WORDS.
SO? EVERYBODY KNOWS BIG WORDS.
WHAT HAPPENED TO MY SHORTS?
YEAH, WELL, WHEN I WAS ONE YEAR OLD, I KNEW THE WORD RHISONOROS!
SO? EVERYBODY KNOWS THAT WORD.
LOOK!
IS IT A TARANTULA?
MAYBE THIS ELASTIC WILL WORK.
OH YEAH? DO YOU KNOW WHAT A RHISONOROS IS?
ARE YOU KIDDING? EVERYBODY KNOWS THAT!
UH-OH.
LET'S GO!

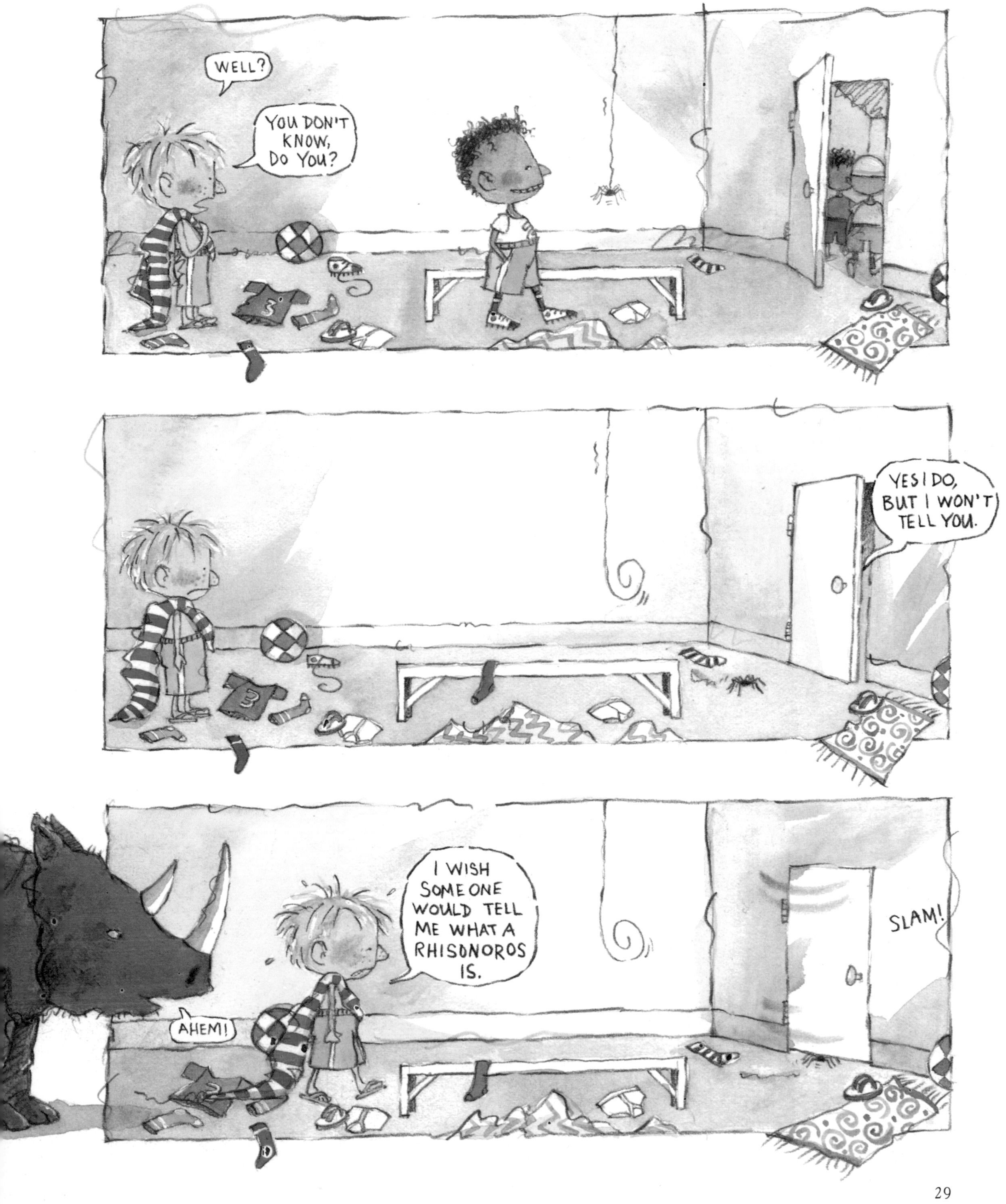
WELL?
YOU DON'T KNOW, DO YOU?
YES I DO, BUT I WON'T TELL YOU.
I WISH SOMEONE WOULD TELL ME WHAT A RHISONOROS IS.
SLAM!
AHEM!

ART?

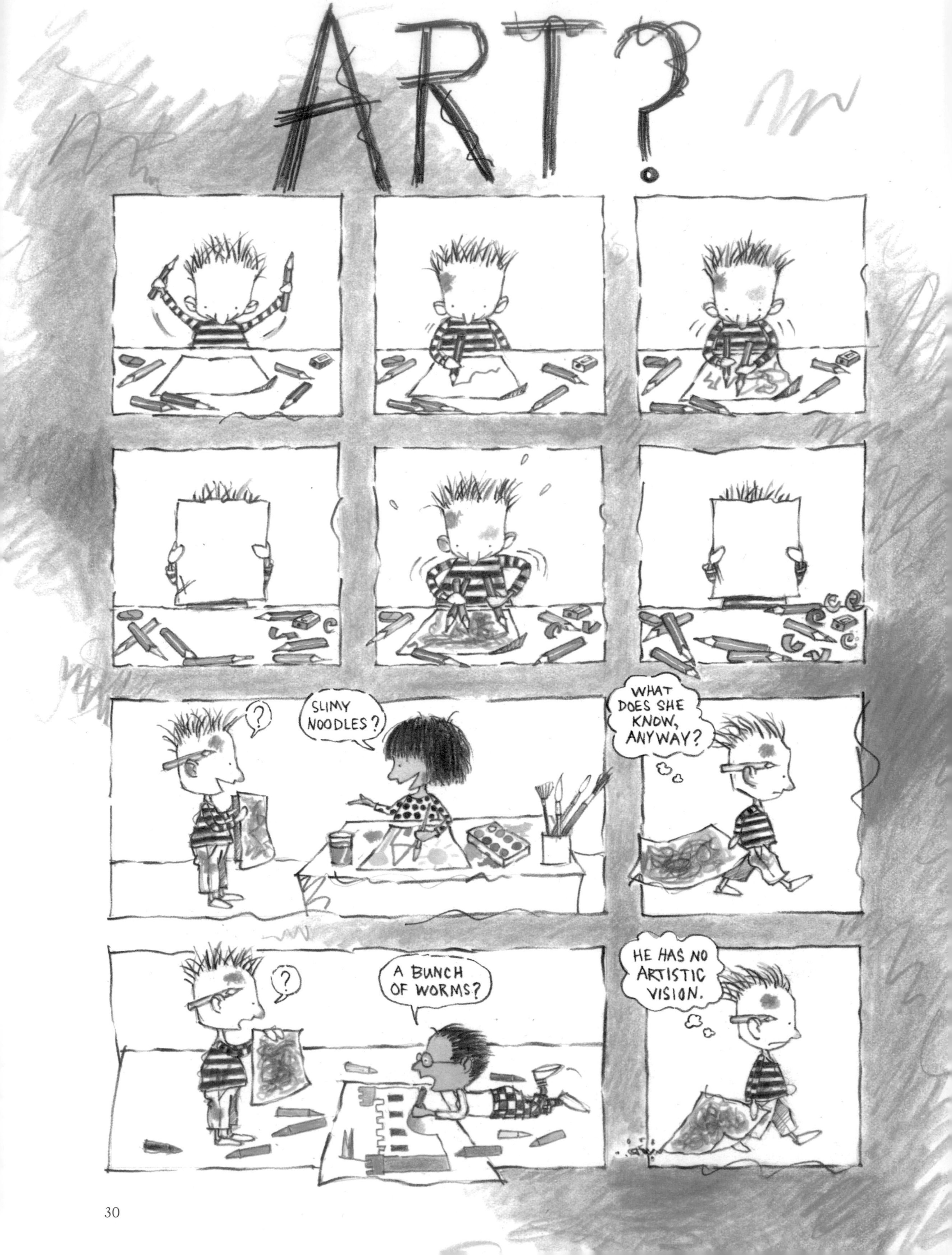
?
SLIMY NOODLES?
WHAT DOES SHE KNOW, ANYWAY?
?
A BUNCH OF WORMS?
HE HAS NO ARTISTIC VISION.

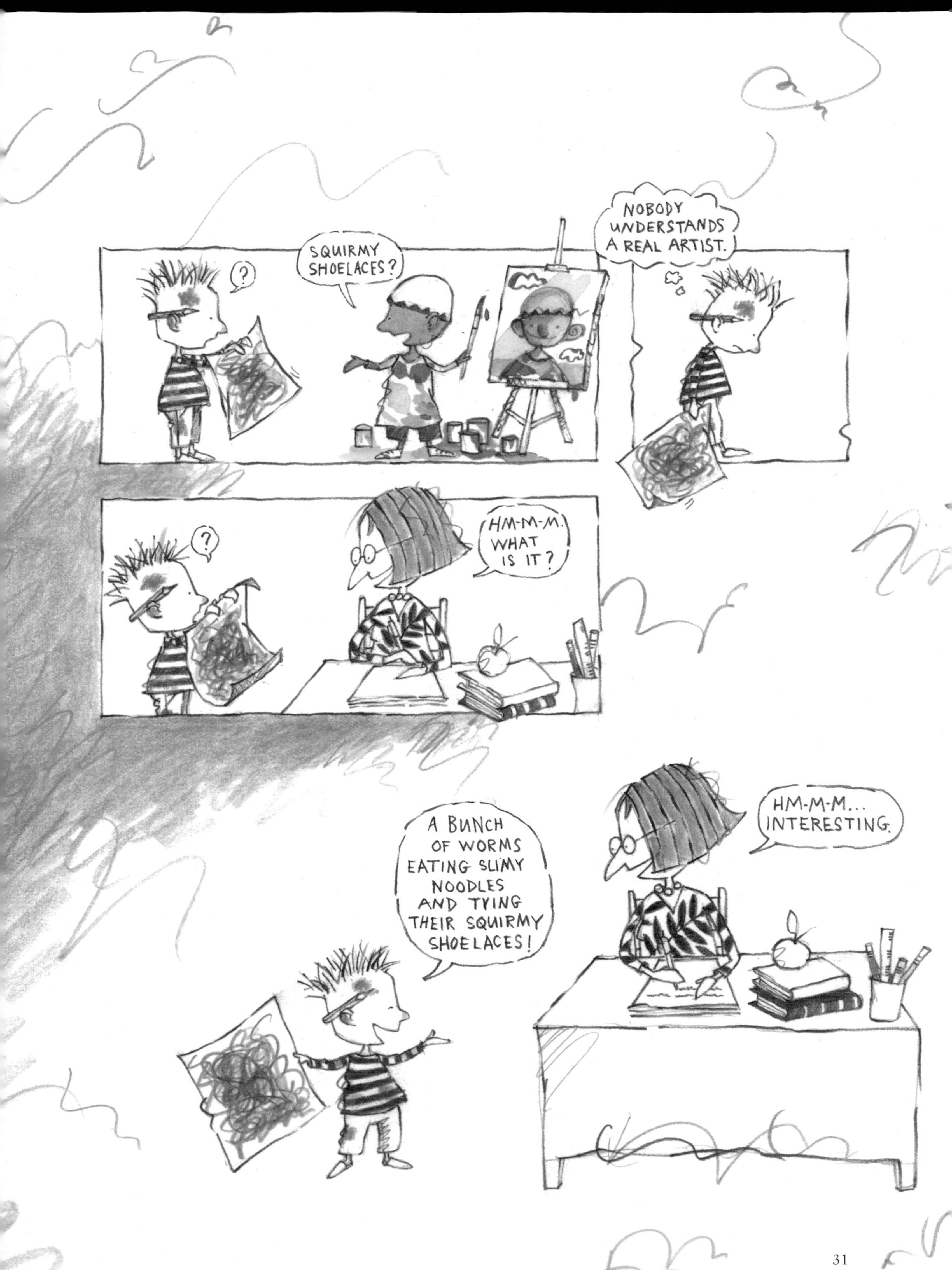
?
SQUIRMY SHOELACES?
NOBODY UNDERSTANDS A REAL ARTIST.
?
HM-M-M. WHAT IS IT?
A BUNCH OF WORMS EATING SLIMY NOODLES AND TYING THEIR SQUIRMY SHOELACES!
HM-M-M... INTERESTING.

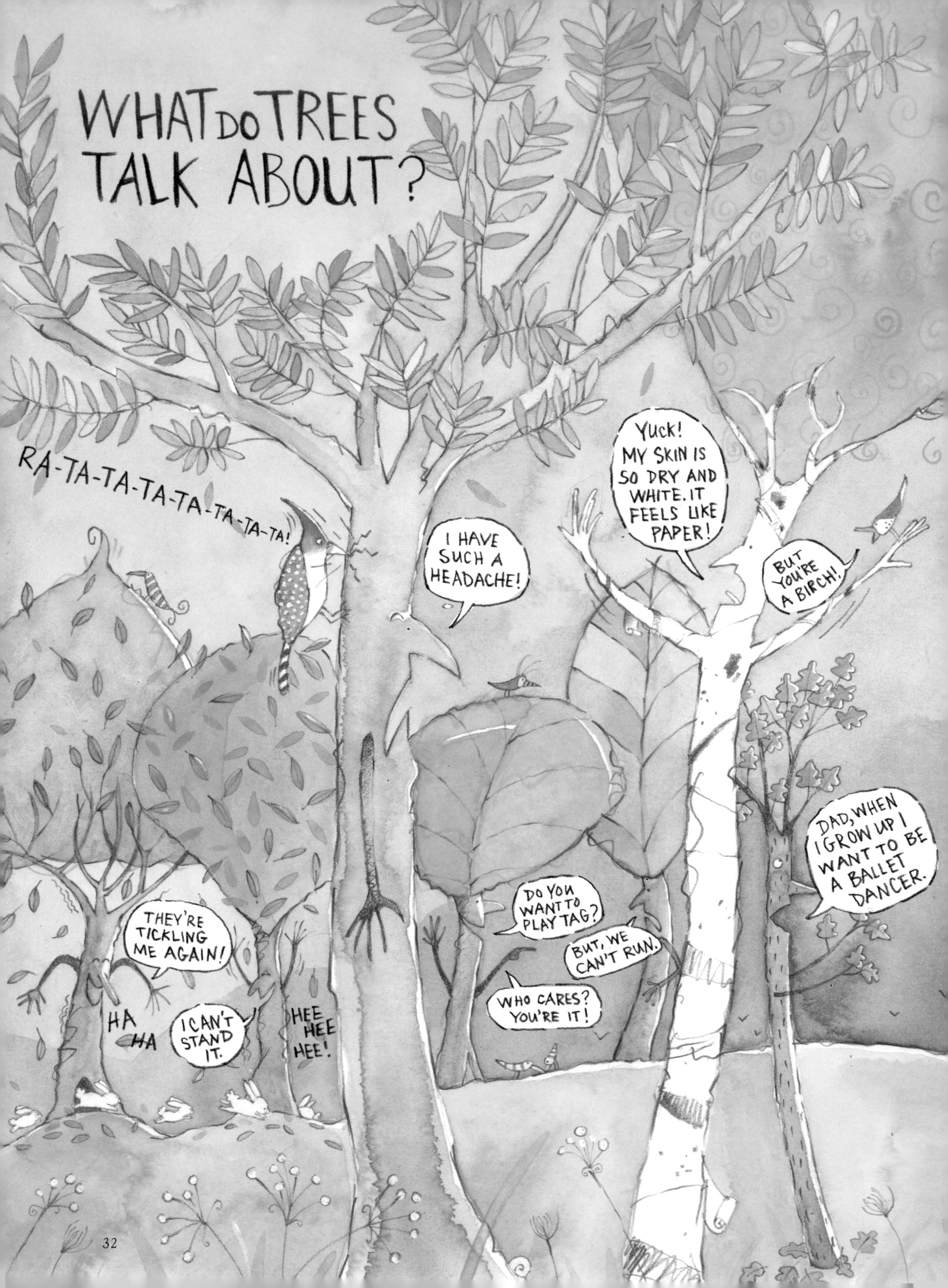
WHAT DO TREES TALK ABOUT?
RA-TA-TA-TA-TA-TA-TA-TA!
I HAVE SUCH A HEADACHE!
YUCK! MY SKIN IS SO DRY AND WHITE. IT FEELS LIKE PAPER!
BUT YOU'RE A BIRCH!
DAD, WHEN I GROW UP I WANT TO BE A BALLET DANCER.
DO YOU WANT TO PLAY TAG?
BUT, WE CAN'T RUN.
WHO CARES? YOU'RE IT!
THEY'RE TICKLING ME AGAIN!
HA HA
I CAN'T STAND IT.
HEE HEE HEE!

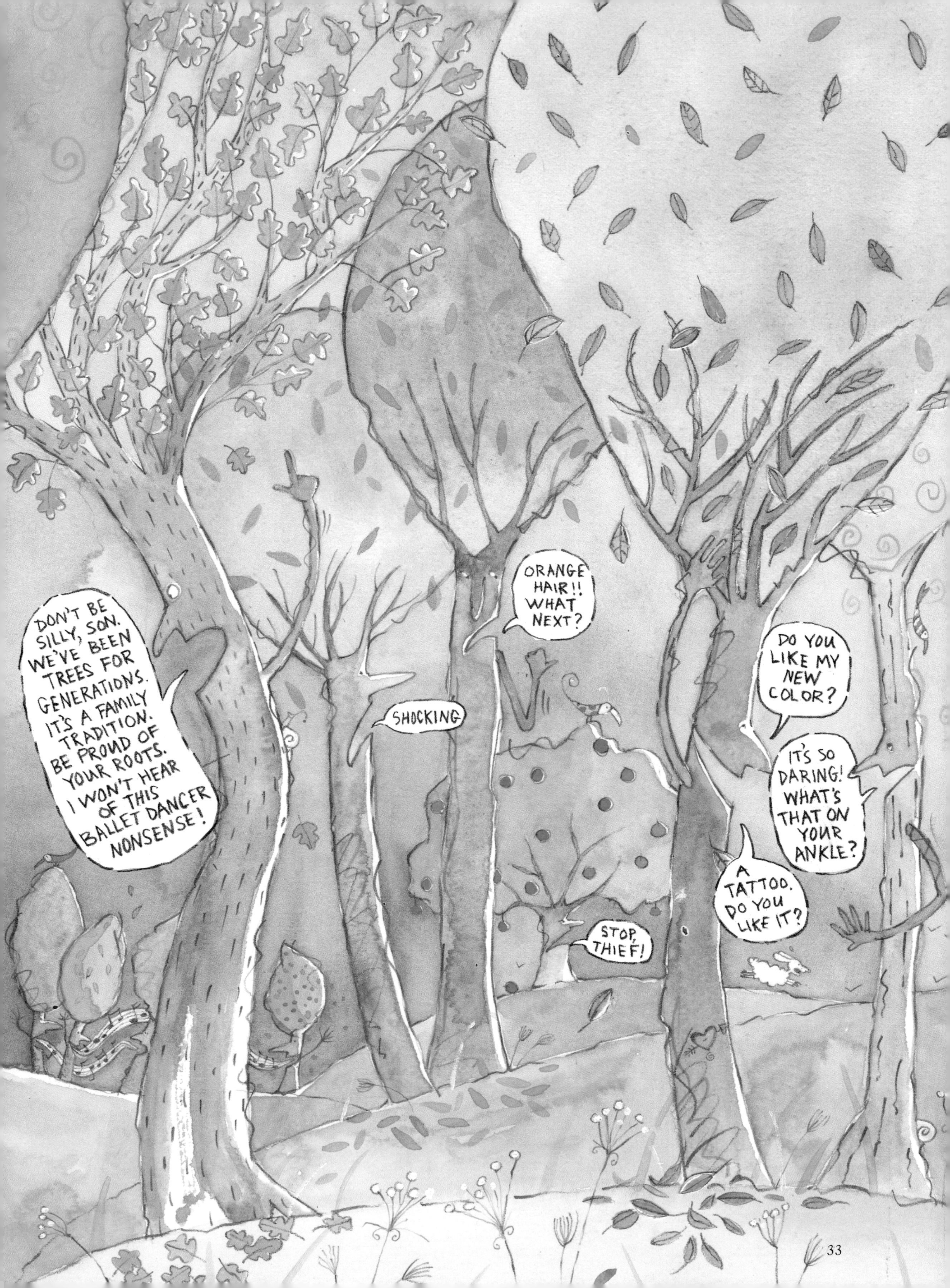
DON'T BE SILLY, SON. WE'VE BEEN TREES FOR GENERATIONS. IT'S A FAMILY TRADITION. BE PROUD OF YOUR ROOTS. I WON'T HEAR OF THIS BALLET DANCER NONSENSE!
SHOCKING
ORANGE HAIR!! WHAT NEXT?
STOP, THIEF!
DO YOU LIKE MY NEW COLOR?
IT'S SO DARING! WHAT'S THAT ON YOUR ANKLE?
A TATTOO. DO YOU LIKE IT?

LIES MY MOTHER TOLD ME

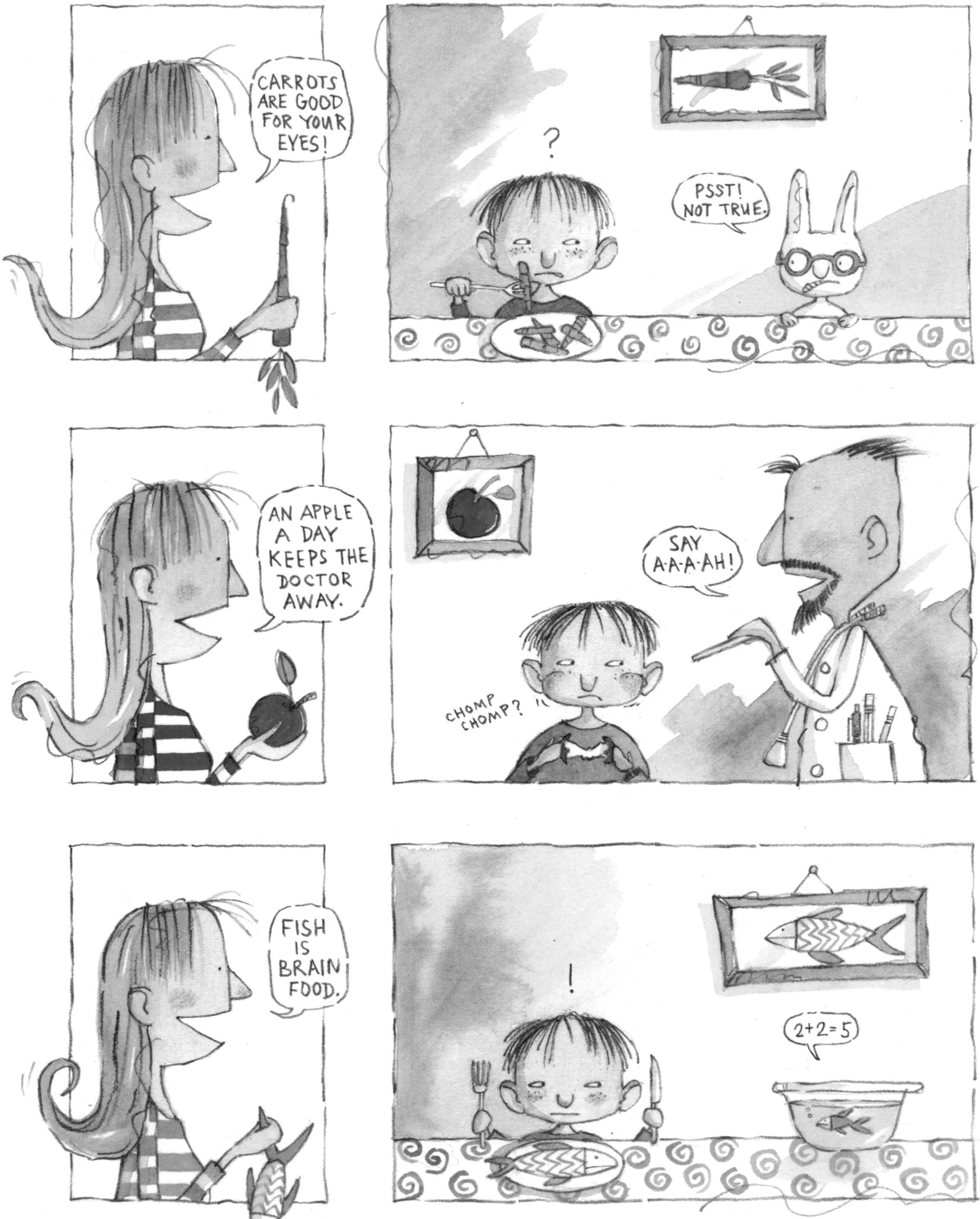

CARROTS ARE GOOD FOR YOUR EYES!
?
PSST! NOT TRUE.
AN APPLE A DAY KEEPS THE DOCTOR AWAY.
SAY A-A-A-AH!
CHOMP CHOMP?
FISH IS BRAIN FOOD.
!
2+2=5

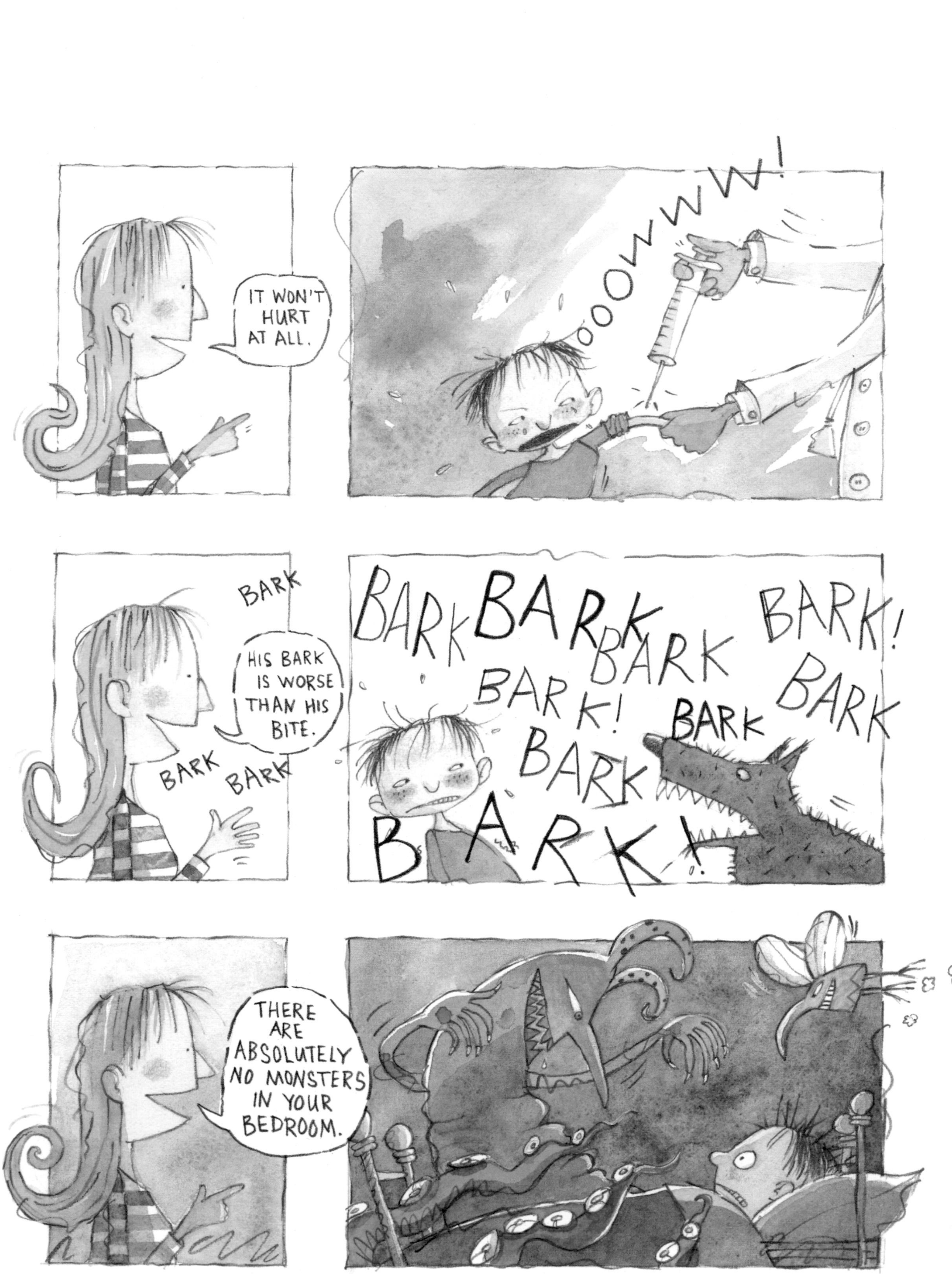
IT WON'T HURT AT ALL.
OOOOWWWW!
BARK
HIS BARK IS WORSE THAN HIS BITE.
BARK
BARK
BARK BARK BARK BARK BARK! BARK! BARK BARK BARK BARK!
THERE ARE ABSOLUTELY NO MONSTERS IN YOUR BEDROOM.

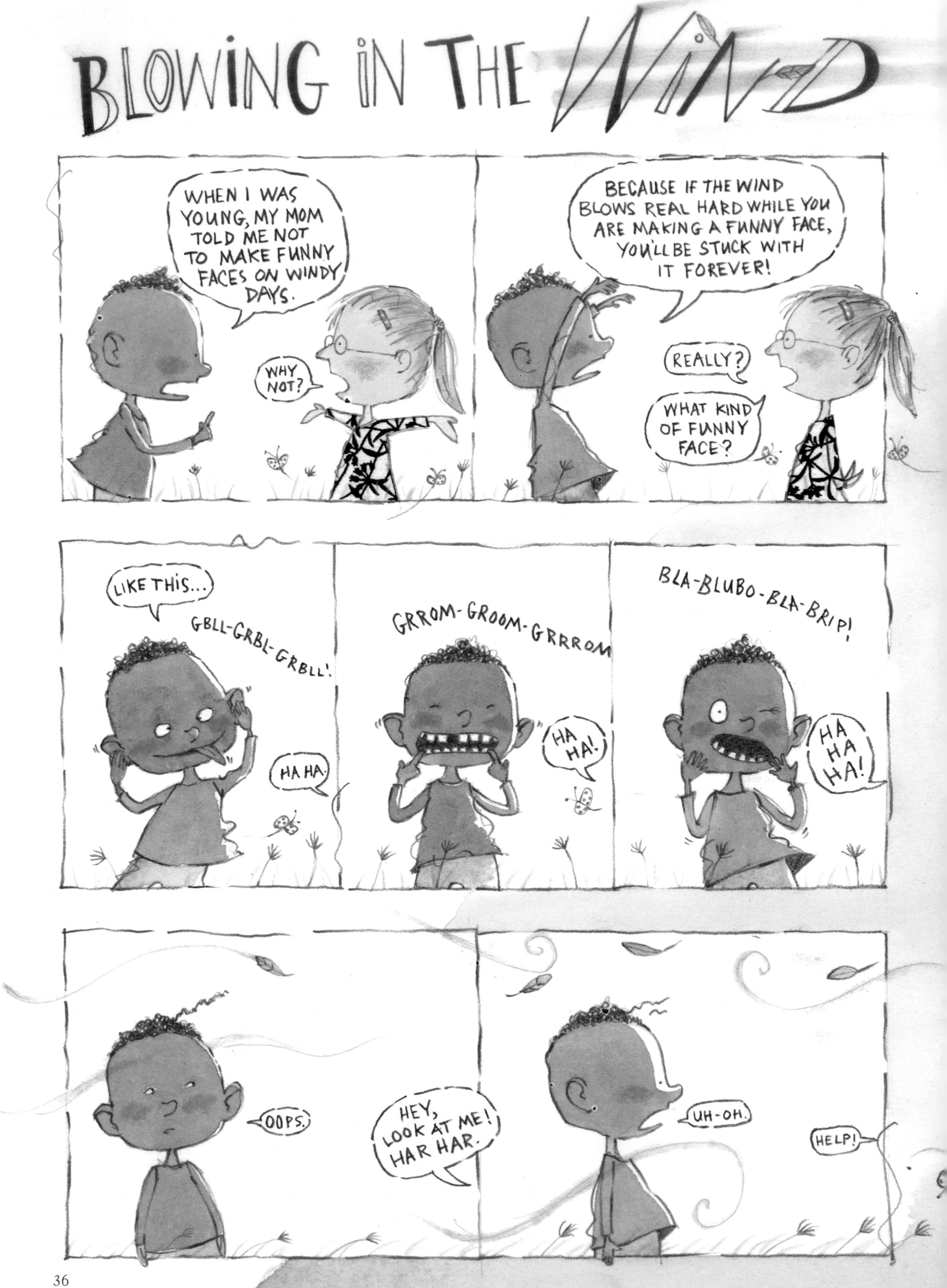
BLOWING IN THE WIND
WHEN I WAS YOUNG, MY MOM TOLD ME NOT TO MAKE FUNNY FACES ON WINDY DAYS.
WHY NOT?
BECAUSE IF THE WIND BLOWS REAL HARD WHILE YOU ARE MAKING A FUNNY FACE, YOU'LL BE STUCK WITH IT FOREVER!
REALLY?
WHAT KIND OF FUNNY FACE?
LIKE THIS...
GBLL-GRBL-GRBLL!
HA HA.
GRROM-GROOM-GRRROM
HA HA!
BLA-BLUBO-BLA-BRIP!
HA HA HA!
OOPS.
HEY, LOOK AT ME! HAR HAR.
UH-OH.
HELP!

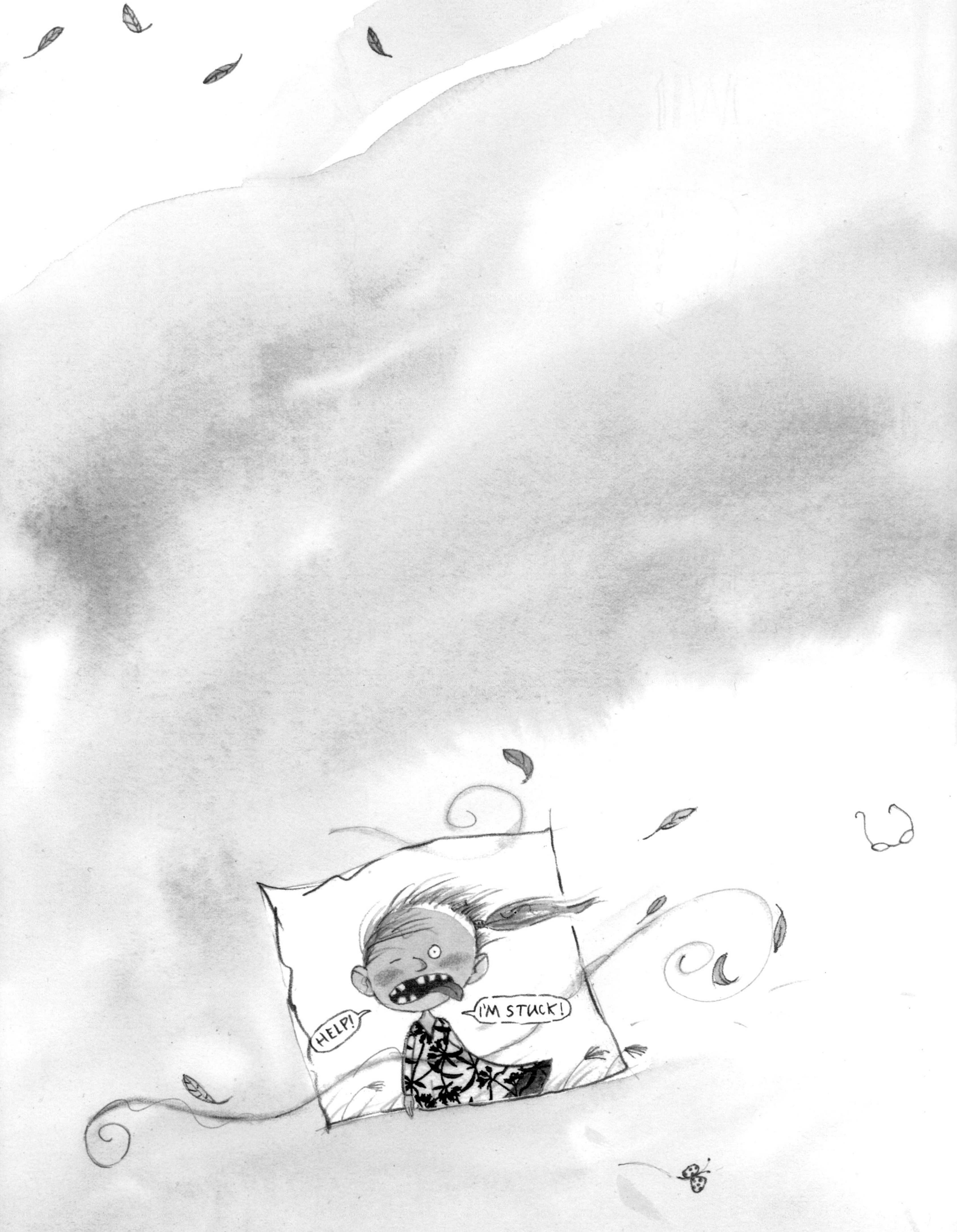
HELP!
I'M STUCK!

The Secret Life of Rabbits

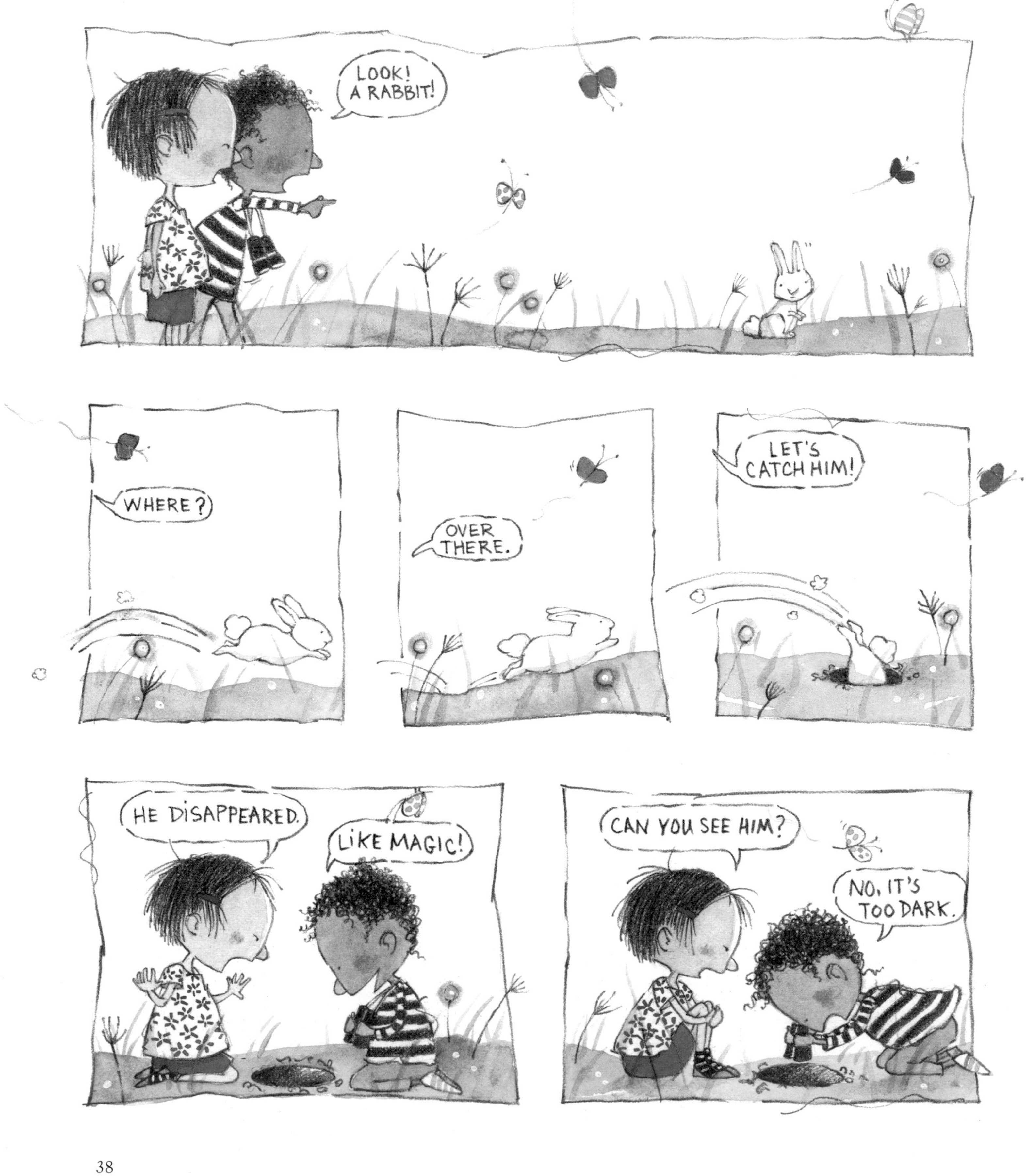
LOOK! A RABBIT!
WHERE?
OVER THERE.
LET'S CATCH HIM!
HE DISAPPEARED.
LIKE MAGIC!
CAN YOU SEE HIM?
NO, IT'S TOO DARK.

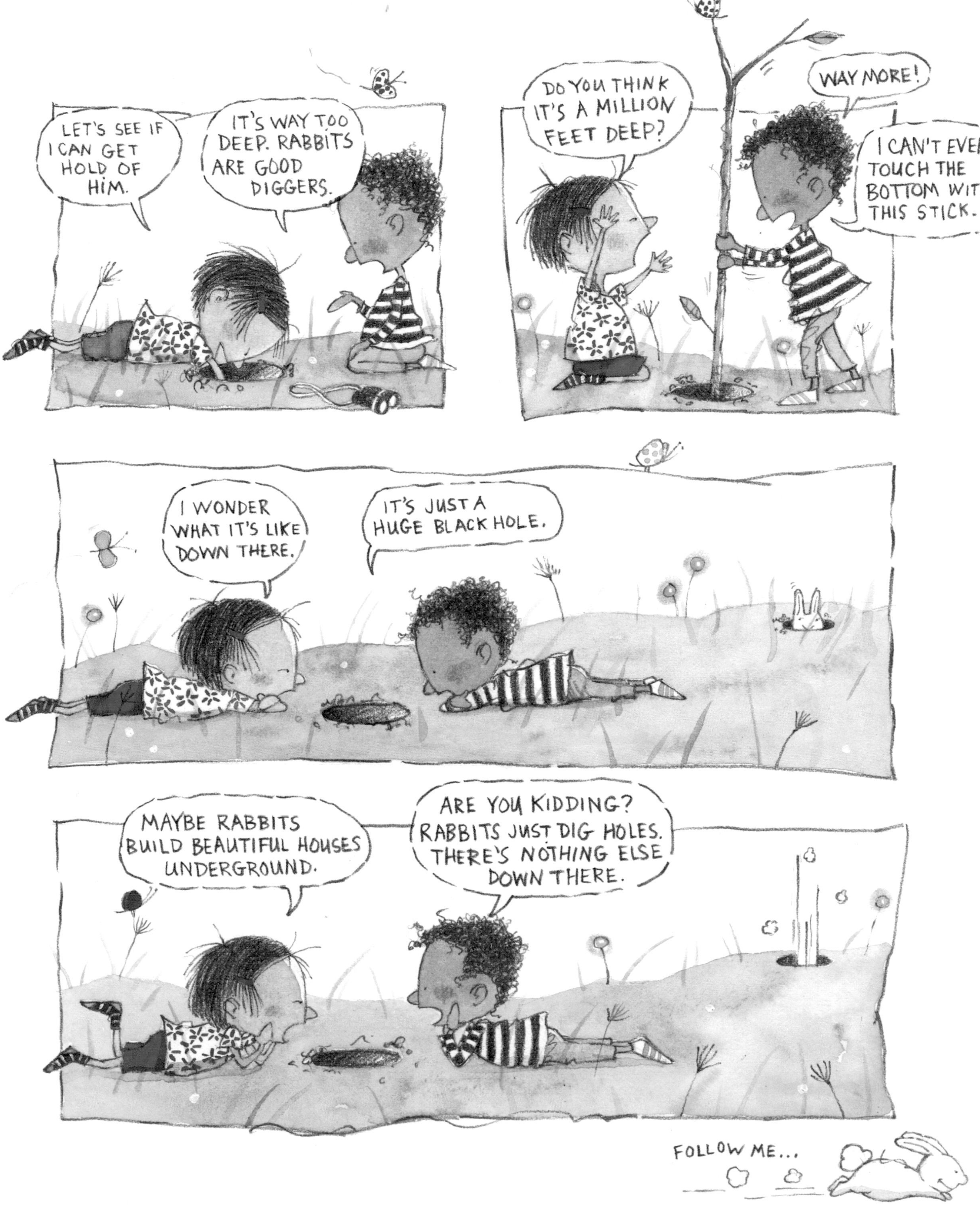
LET'S SEE IF I CAN GET HOLD OF HIM.
IT'S WAY TOO DEEP. RABBITS ARE GOOD DIGGERS.
DO YOU THINK IT'S A MILLION FEET DEEP?
WAY MORE!
I CAN'T EVEN TOUCH THE BOTTOM WITH THIS STICK.
I WONDER WHAT IT'S LIKE DOWN THERE.
IT'S JUST A HUGE BLACK HOLE.
MAYBE RABBITS BUILD BEAUTIFUL HOUSES UNDERGROUND.
ARE YOU KIDDING? RABBITS JUST DIG HOLES. THERE'S NOTHING ELSE DOWN THERE.
FOLLOW ME...

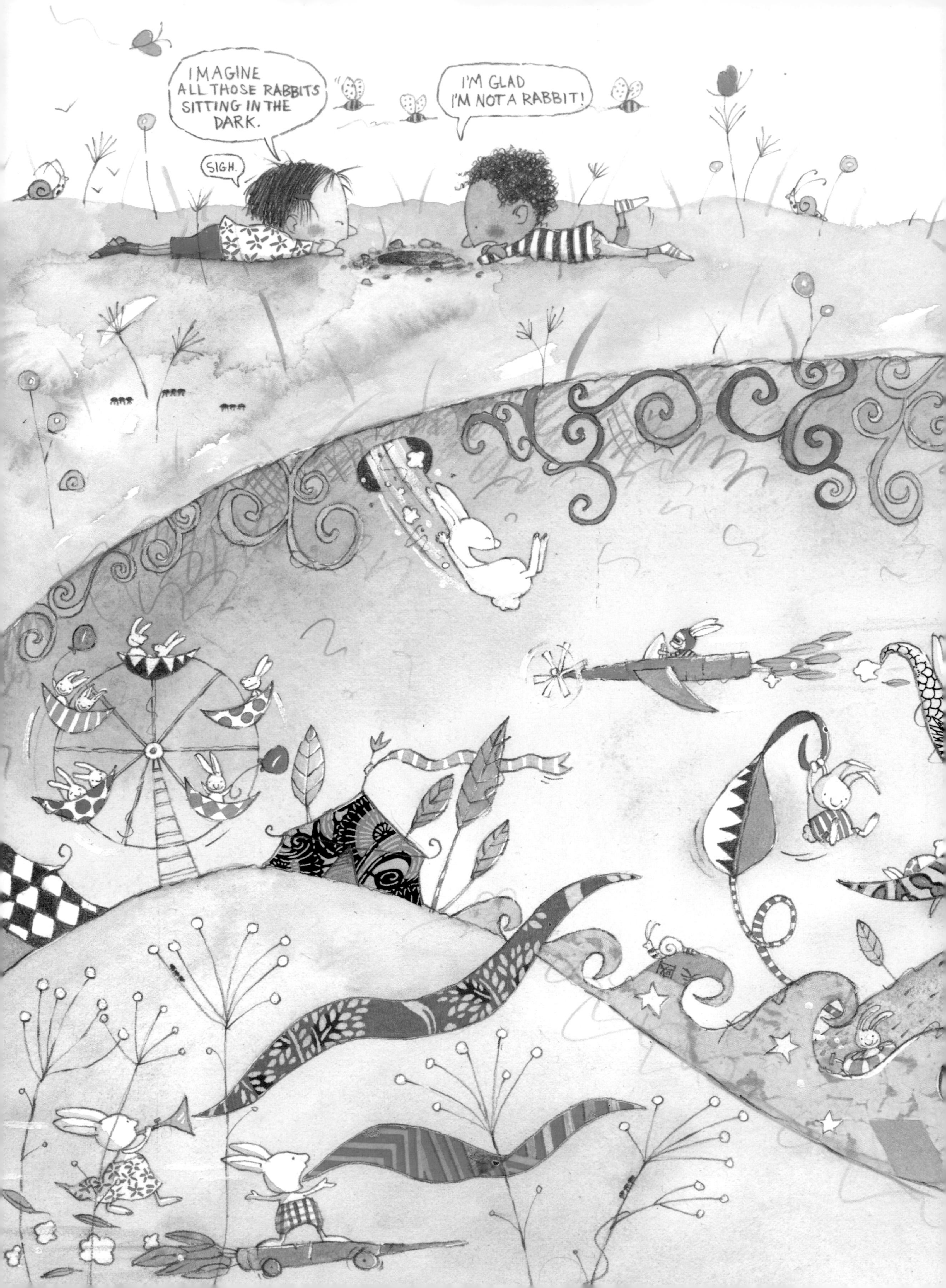

IMAGINE ALL THOSE RABBITS SITTING IN THE DARK.
SIGH.
I'M GLAD I'M NOT A RABBIT!

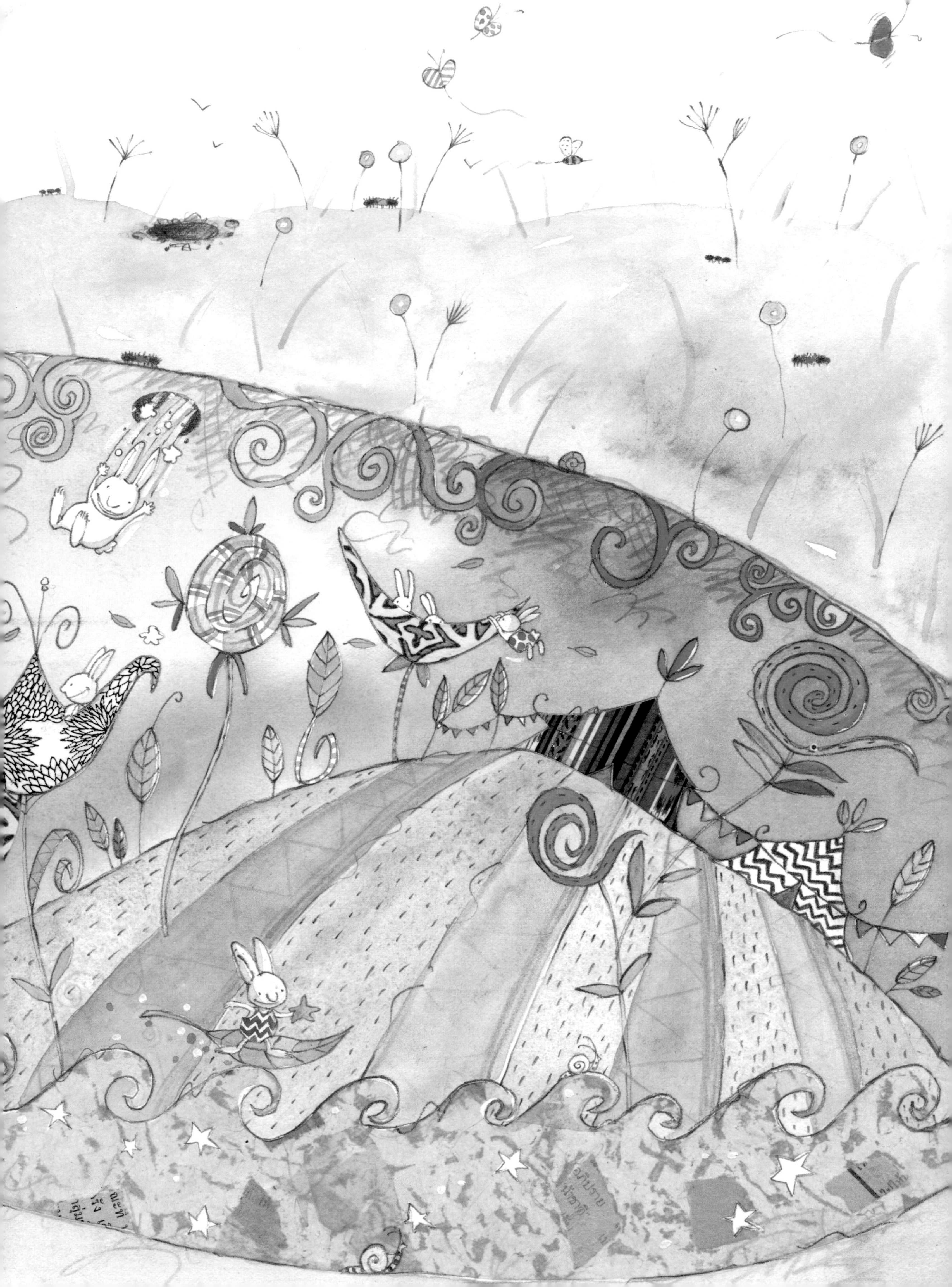

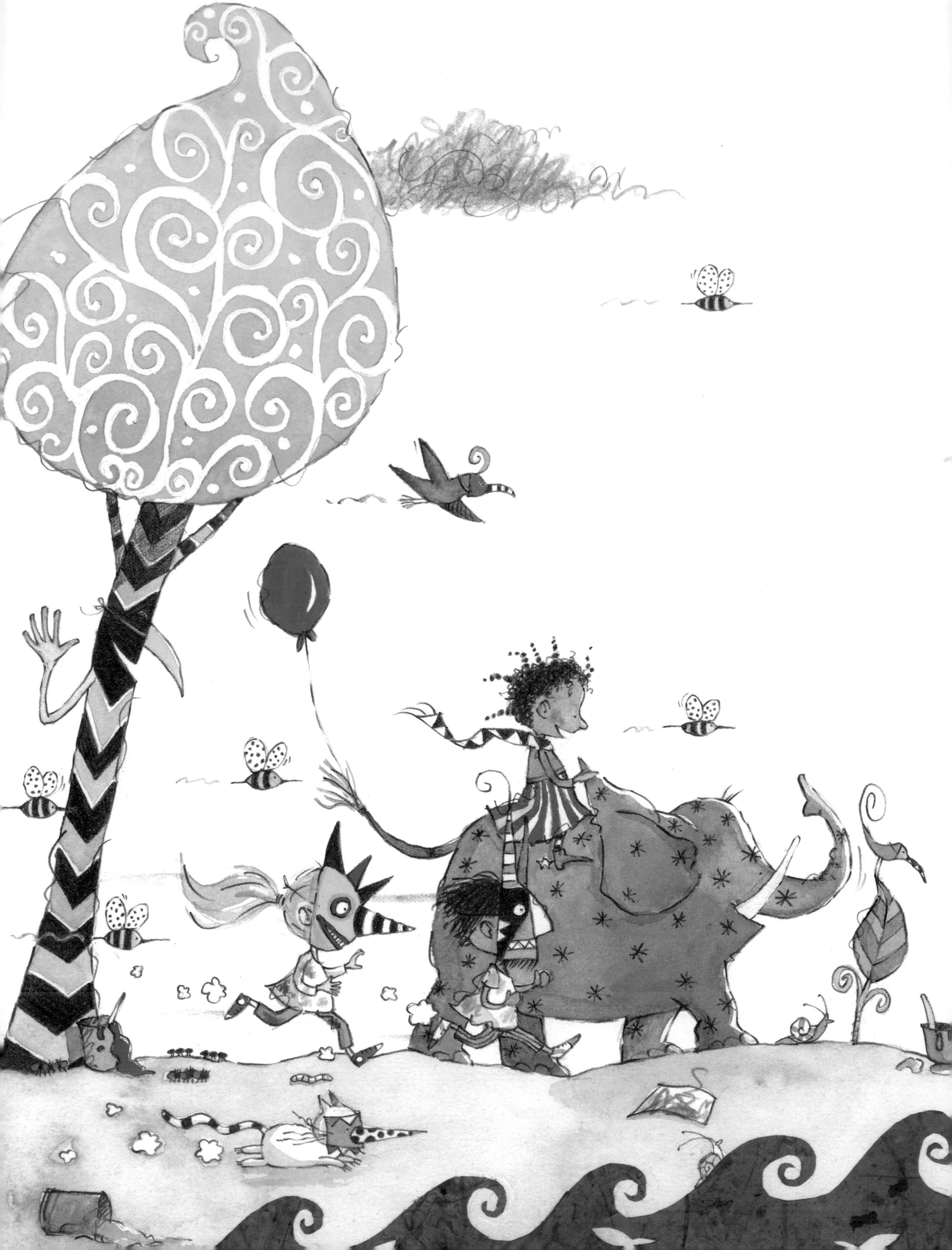